CITY OF BONES

(An Ava Gold Mystery—Book Three)

BLAKE PIERCE

Blake Pierce

Blake Pierce is the USA Today bestselling author of the RILEY PAGE mystery series, which includes seventeen books. Blake Pierce is also the author of the MACKENZIE WHITE mystery series, comprising fourteen books; of the AVERY BLACK mystery series, comprising six books; of the KERI LOCKE mystery series, comprising five books; of the MAKING OF RILEY PAIGE mystery series, comprising six books; of the KATE WISE mystery series, comprising seven books; of the CHLOE FINE psychological suspense mystery, comprising six books; of the JESSE HUNT psychological suspense thriller series, comprising nineteen books; of the AU PAIR psychological suspense thriller series, comprising three books; of the ZOE PRIME mystery series, comprising six books; of the ADELE SHARP mystery series, comprising thirteen books, of the EUROPEAN VOYAGE cozy mystery series, comprising four books; of the new LAURA FROST FBI suspense thriller, comprising six books (and counting); of the new ELLA DARK FBI suspense thriller, comprising nine books (and counting); of the A YEAR IN EUROPE cozy mystery series, comprising nine books, of the AVA GOLD mystery series, comprising six books (and counting); and of the RACHEL GIFT mystery series, comprising six books (and counting).

An avid reader and lifelong fan of the mystery and thriller genres, Blake loves to hear from you, so please feel free to visit www.blakepierceauthor.com to learn more and stay in touch.

BOOKS BY BLAKE PIERCE

RACHEL GIFT MYSTERY SERIES
HER LAST WISH (Book #1)
HER LAST CHANCE (Book #2)
HER LAST HOPE (Book #3)
HER LAST FEAR (Book #4)
HER LAST CHOICE (Book #5)
HER LAST BREATH (Book #6)

AVA GOLD MYSTERY SERIES
CITY OF PREY (Book #1)
CITY OF FEAR (Book #2)
CITY OF BONES (Book #3)
CITY OF GHOSTS (Book #4)
CITY OF DEATH (Book #5)
CITY OF VICE (Book #6)

A YEAR IN EUROPE
A MURDER IN PARIS (Book #1)
DEATH IN FLORENCE (Book #2)
VENGEANCE IN VIENNA (Book #3)
A FATALITY IN SPAIN (Book #4)

ELLA DARK FBI SUSPENSE THRILLER
GIRL, ALONE (Book #1)
GIRL, TAKEN (Book #2)
GIRL, HUNTED (Book #3)
GIRL, SILENCED (Book #4)
GIRL, VANISHED (Book 5)
GIRL ERASED (Book #6)
GIRL, FORSAKEN (Book #7)
GIRL, TRAPPED (Book #8)
GIRL, EXPENDABLE (Book #9)

LAURA FROST FBI SUSPENSE THRILLER
ALREADY GONE (Book #1)
ALREADY SEEN (Book #2)

ALREADY TRAPPED (Book #3)
ALREADY MISSING (Book #4)
ALREADY DEAD (Book #5)
ALREADY TAKEN (Book #6)

EUROPEAN VOYAGE COZY MYSTERY SERIES
MURDER (AND BAKLAVA) (Book #1)
DEATH (AND APPLE STRUDEL) (Book #2)
CRIME (AND LAGER) (Book #3)
MISFORTUNE (AND GOUDA) (Book #4)
CALAMITY (AND A DANISH) (Book #5)
MAYHEM (AND HERRING) (Book #6)

ADELE SHARP MYSTERY SERIES
LEFT TO DIE (Book #1)
LEFT TO RUN (Book #2)
LEFT TO HIDE (Book #3)
LEFT TO KILL (Book #4)
LEFT TO MURDER (Book #5)
LEFT TO ENVY (Book #6)
LEFT TO LAPSE (Book #7)
LEFT TO VANISH (Book #8)
LEFT TO HUNT (Book #9)
LEFT TO FEAR (Book #10)
LEFT TO PREY (Book #11)
LEFT TO LURE (Book #12)
LEFT TO CRAVE (Book #13)

THE AU PAIR SERIES
ALMOST GONE (Book#1)
ALMOST LOST (Book #2)
ALMOST DEAD (Book #3)

ZOE PRIME MYSTERY SERIES
FACE OF DEATH (Book#1)
FACE OF MURDER (Book #2)
FACE OF FEAR (Book #3)
FACE OF MADNESS (Book #4)
FACE OF FURY (Book #5)
FACE OF DARKNESS (Book #6)

A JESSIE HUNT PSYCHOLOGICAL SUSPENSE SERIES
THE PERFECT WIFE (Book #1)
THE PERFECT BLOCK (Book #2)
THE PERFECT HOUSE (Book #3)
THE PERFECT SMILE (Book #4)
THE PERFECT LIE (Book #5)
THE PERFECT LOOK (Book #6)
THE PERFECT AFFAIR (Book #7)
THE PERFECT ALIBI (Book #8)
THE PERFECT NEIGHBOR (Book #9)
THE PERFECT DISGUISE (Book #10)
THE PERFECT SECRET (Book #11)
THE PERFECT FAÇADE (Book #12)
THE PERFECT IMPRESSION (Book #13)
THE PERFECT DECEIT (Book #14)
THE PERFECT MISTRESS (Book #15)
THE PERFECT IMAGE (Book #16)
THE PERFECT VEIL (Book #17)
THE PERFECT INDISCRETION (Book #18)
THE PERFECT RUMOR (Book #19)

CHLOE FINE PSYCHOLOGICAL SUSPENSE SERIES
NEXT DOOR (Book #1)
A NEIGHBOR'S LIE (Book #2)
CUL DE SAC (Book #3)
SILENT NEIGHBOR (Book #4)
HOMECOMING (Book #5)
TINTED WINDOWS (Book #6)

KATE WISE MYSTERY SERIES
IF SHE KNEW (Book #1)
IF SHE SAW (Book #2)
IF SHE RAN (Book #3)
IF SHE HID (Book #4)
IF SHE FLED (Book #5)
IF SHE FEARED (Book #6)
IF SHE HEARD (Book #7)

THE MAKING OF RILEY PAIGE SERIES

WATCHING (Book #1)
WAITING (Book #2)
LURING (Book #3)
TAKING (Book #4)
STALKING (Book #5)
KILLING (Book #6)

RILEY PAIGE MYSTERY SERIES
ONCE GONE (Book #1)
ONCE TAKEN (Book #2)
ONCE CRAVED (Book #3)
ONCE LURED (Book #4)
ONCE HUNTED (Book #5)
ONCE PINED (Book #6)
ONCE FORSAKEN (Book #7)
ONCE COLD (Book #8)
ONCE STALKED (Book #9)
ONCE LOST (Book #10)
ONCE BURIED (Book #11)
ONCE BOUND (Book #12)
ONCE TRAPPED (Book #13)
ONCE DORMANT (Book #14)
ONCE SHUNNED (Book #15)
ONCE MISSED (Book #16)
ONCE CHOSEN (Book #17)

MACKENZIE WHITE MYSTERY SERIES
BEFORE HE KILLS (Book #1)
BEFORE HE SEES (Book #2)
BEFORE HE COVETS (Book #3)
BEFORE HE TAKES (Book #4)
BEFORE HE NEEDS (Book #5)
BEFORE HE FEELS (Book #6)
BEFORE HE SINS (Book #7)
BEFORE HE HUNTS (Book #8)
BEFORE HE PREYS (Book #9)
BEFORE HE LONGS (Book #10)
BEFORE HE LAPSES (Book #11)
BEFORE HE ENVIES (Book #12)
BEFORE HE STALKS (Book #13)

BEFORE HE HARMS (Book #14)

AVERY BLACK MYSTERY SERIES
CAUSE TO KILL (Book #1)
CAUSE TO RUN (Book #2)
CAUSE TO HIDE (Book #3)
CAUSE TO FEAR (Book #4)
CAUSE TO SAVE (Book #5)
CAUSE TO DREAD (Book #6)

KERI LOCKE MYSTERY SERIES
A TRACE OF DEATH (Book #1)
A TRACE OF MURDER (Book #2)
A TRACE OF VICE (Book #3)
A TRACE OF CRIME (Book #4)
A TRACE OF HOPE (Book #5)

PROLOGUE

Millie Newsom kept hearing how the world was changing for the better but she'd be damned if she'd seen much of it. She still felt like a second-class citizen as she walked down the street mainly just because she was a woman. Based on the mindsets and debates taking place all around New York City, Millie thought the day would eventually come when women were seen as equals, but she doubted she'd see it in her lifetime.

Her job was a good example of this. She'd been a reporter for two years now and even though she was among the best for her paper, she was not viewed as just a journalist, but a *woman* journalist—as if having breasts made her any worse or better of a journalist than a man. Still, she knew she was lucky to have the job because journalism, just like any other profession, was predominately occupied by men.

Millie was not quite a household name, not even among those who made it a point to read the papers on a daily basis. But enough people in her own paper and the competing rags knew about her. She was good at her job and though it seemed to pain some to admit it, she knew it was true. She used this confidence to keep her step straight and her mind at ease as she walked down the Brooklyn streets at 5:15, crossing the road and doing her best to blend in. It was a bit harder here in Brooklyn than in some of the busier areas in the city. Brooklyn had a new and exciting feel to it as it seemed to grow day by day, but it still lacked the bustle and vibrancy she was accustomed to closer to Manhattan.

Millie had dressed as plainly as possible, as to not draw attention to herself. She'd been assigned to tail a known mob member, hoping to crack open a story about the mob's alleged success in bootlegging operations. She looked ahead and saw her target at the end of the block. He was in a hurry and had his head pointed straight ahead. Millie tried her best to keep a steady pace, wanting to stay just far enough behind the mafioso so he would not see her, but close enough so that she did not lose him.

1

"Millie! Hey, Millie!"

The whispered mention of her name from behind her both scared and irritated her. She paused for a moment and looked behind her. A thin and far-too-young-looking man was following behind her. His name was Ronald Amberley, a promising young journalist that the editors of the paper had asked to trail along behind her. They claimed it was so he could learn from her, but she couldn't help but wonder if it was to covertly attach a male presence to her successes. She hadn't liked the idea at first but she knew it made sense.

She was, after all, a rather attractive blonde woman who was tailing the mob. Having some sort of masculine presence was a good idea even if he *was* rail thin and his patchy beard made him look like a boy trying to play the part of an adult. Yes, Ronald was getting his training. But really, he was only slowing her down.

"What is it, Ronald?" she said as he caught up to her.

"Don't you think you're moving too fast?"

"No. He's almost an entire block ahead of me. Keep up."

"But if you—"

She glared at him and shook her head, taking perhaps a bit too much joy out of the startled look that came across his face. Ronald knew how quietly respected and revered she was back at the paper. She was twenty-eight years old and had her entire career ahead of her. She was doing her best to follow in the footsteps of her hero, Elizabeth Jane Cochran, one of the first influential female journalists who had also just happened to travel the globe in seventy-two days in an effort to show Jules Verne it could, in fact, be done. And while Millie knew it was foolish to dream of a global adventure, she thought it might be possible to attain the same levels of success Elizabeth Cochran had achieved.

If she was able to blow this story open, it would be a huge step toward that goal, that was for sure. And the key to it possibly rested with the mafioso ahead of her. She watched him closely as he turned right, heading down a different street. A few people were walking between them, giving her ample cover as she quickly followed along behind him. She was also aware of Ronald trailing her. When this was all over, she supposed the first thing she'd have to properly train him on was how to remain discreet while tailing someone.

She looked back quickly, just to make sure he hadn't gotten separated from her before she took the same corner she saw the mob guy disappear behind. Ronald was still back there, struggling to keep up while also trying to blend in. If anything, it looked like he might be stalking her—which wasn't going to help them blend in either.

When Millie turned back around to locate the mafioso again, she saw that he had stopped. Not only that, but he was looking right at her. Reacting as quickly as she could, Millie halted in her tracks and, thank God above, spotted the newsstand directly to her right, just at the edge of the sidewalk.

She leaned slightly toward it and reached for one of today's papers. She tried to keep her gaze on the mafioso out of the corner of her eye, but he was just out of sight. As she pretended to eye the newspaper, now also attracting the attention of the paper salesman, she was worried that her cover was going to be blown. Even if she managed to keep her cool, Lord only knew how Ronald would react when he came up on her and saw that he had potentially been spotted.

What to do? she asked herself. *What to do, what to d—*

A shot rang out. It was clear and very close, the unmistakable sound of gunfire.

It was just a single report, but it sent the streets into a flurry of activity. First of all, it caused Millie to jump away from the newsstand, her head swiveling first in the direction she thought the shot had come from, and then in search of Ronald.

She didn't see Ronald, though. There were too many people currently running for cover at the sound of the gunshot. Women were screaming and shouts of concern came from every direction. Millie lifted her right foot to start running to where she hoped Ronald would appear around the corner any minute, but lifting her leg suddenly seemed very difficult.

It was then that she felt a cold nagging feeling just below her chest. She looked down and saw a bright red spot in the checkered print of her coat. Just as she saw it, Ronald appeared around the edge of the building beside her. When he saw her, his eyes, already wide from the sound of gunfire, grew even wider when he spotted the still-blossoming bloodstain below her left breast.

"Ronald…"

"My God, Millie!" He came rushing forward just as she started to feel herself fall to the ground. Her knees gave way and she went down hard. She was pretty sure Ronald caught her as she fell, but her head was turned the other way. The last thing she saw before the darkness took her was the mafioso escaping quickly through the panicked crowd.

CHAPTER ONE

Ava Gold stared at the run-down building in front of her, trying to determine what it had been used for. It had the look of a dodgy bar of some kind, not quite large enough to make it as a club. Of course, bars weren't around anymore thanks to the much-griped-about stranglehold of prohibition. But she could imagine this place as having once catered to heavy drinkers and men just anxious for some time away from their wives and kids. It was a simple one-story affair, made of wood and old brick. There was an overall seedy feel to it, especially in the darkness of night, the sort of place that kept secrets.

In that regard, it made sense that she'd ended up here. Ava had been following a loose lead concerning Clarence's death for five days now. It had started with looking into old cases where a criminal had gone free and any description of a man of short stature wearing a wide-brimmed hat low on his head. It was the depiction of the man who had killed Clarence, as well as that of a man who got away with another shooting just a week or so before.

A few quick interviews with eyewitnesses and some cross-referencing of old police records had led her here. The old, faded letters above the door read **Clancy's**, and the broken windows and boarded-over door spoke of a place that had not been open for at least several months. But based on some of the intel she'd gotten from some of her jazz-playing friends, the old place was used for a number of nefarious purposes.

Clancy's sat dead center of an equally tired and dusty street. Currently, at nine o'clock at night, the street was practically empty. She'd wanted to be there earlier but had made sure to make it home in time to put Jeffrey to bed. She was by herself, as this was not an official case. In fact, she figured Frank would lose his mind if he knew what she was about to do.

You're thinking a lot about Frank, aren't you? she asked herself. She supposed she was, but that was to be expected. After all, they were having dinner later tonight. They were supposed to meet half an hour from now, but she wasn't sure if it was going to work out that way. This private case might make a good excuse to miss it. She knew she

4

should have told him no when he asked, but she thought it might come off as rude.

"Focus," she told herself. Then, pushing thoughts of the coming (and surely awkward) dinner with Frank out of her head, she hurried across the street. She made sure to stick to the shadows along the side of the building, slinking into an old alleyway that smelled of urine and dust. She slowed her pace, keeping her head close to the wall. She looked for a side entrance but didn't see one. It was so dark in the alley that she had to run her hands along the brick to make sure she didn't miss a way in.

When she came to the back of the building, she found another alley that ran along behind the row of failed businesses along the street. It was separated by a lot that seemed to currently be in development for something. She studied the rear of Clancy's and saw a small wooden door that had once served as its rear entrance. She then looked down the alleyway, hoping to see an automobile to give her some idea if there was anyone here or not. As it was, the night was too dark and the alleyway too long for her to see much of anything.

Not that it mattered. As she neared the door, she heard a woman's voice. It was soft and happy. It almost like a flirtatious murmur, though the door made it hard to tell. This wasn't too much of a stretch, as she'd heard that one of the many forms of entertainment that took place in the old back room of Clancy's was prostitution. From the start, Ava figured that was going to be her way in. It's why she'd dolled herself up so foolishly before leaving the apartment. Her face was pristinely powdered, her makeup applied with real intent for the first time since Clarence passed away. She'd done the best she could with her hair, though it had never really been manageable. But she didn't think it would matter, given the dress she was wearing under her coat. It didn't leave much to the imagination and, despite the reason for wearing it, had her feeling rather lovely.

Making sure her gun was tucked securely away beneath her coat, Ava approached the door and knocked. She found that she was surprisingly calm as she waited. The female murmuring from inside came to a stop and there was silence for a while. She knocked again and this time she heard the shuffling of footsteps right away. She also heard the clinking of a few bottles, which was always a damning noise in the prohibition era.

"Yeah, who's it?" came a slurred male voice. Apparently, he'd been enjoying some of what was in those bottles.

5

"Um, I'm Rosie," she said, putting on a quiet, ultra-feminine voice. "I was told to come here for some work."

There was the slightest bit of hesitation before the door opened, but only a bit. A man with a broad face peered out. The one eye Ava saw widened when it saw her. The door opened a bit more but then stopped.

"Who sent you?"

Here, she was going to have to lie and hope there had been enough drinking to help sway the man's judgment. "My friend Esther told me to come. She said it would be okay. She said Tony Two told her to send some of her friends."

She had no idea if notorious mobster Tony Two had dealings here or not. But Ava had already been placed in his bad graces so she figured this little misuse of his name and stature couldn't hurt.

Apparently, it worked. The door opened and the man greeted her with a wide smile. He made no attempt to hide that he was checking her out. "You know Tony Two personally?"

"No. Just heard about him. I think Esther might know him." This was absolutely not true at all. She didn't even know an Esther; she'd pulled the name from a police report from a few months back.

"And you...you're uh, looking for work?"

"I am." She gave her best flirtatious smile and unbuttoned her coat to let him get a peek at the dress beneath. It was cut low and pushed her breasts up in a way that, to her, seemed foolish. Jesus, men were stupid.

"Oh, well them come on in. We've got some customers headed over in just a second. In the meantime, maybe I can get to know you a bit."

He opened the door for her and allowed her to pass inside. She instantly started to scan the place. She entered into a sizable room with two doors, one on both sides. Sitting against the back wall was a plush, well-worn chair. Currently, a blonde woman wearing an outfit that made Ava's dress look like church-wear was straddling a man in a suit. Ava doubted she was any older than twenty. The woman smiled widely at Ava and nodded as if they were in some sort of secret club. She turned her attention back to the man, whispering things into his ear.

Behind her, the door closed and, within an instant, the man who had answered it grabbed Ava on her backside. She was almost thankful for it, as it gave her a suitable reason to go ahead and get to the point of why she was here.

The moment his inappropriate squeeze was done, Ava reached around and grabbed the hand that had squeezed her. She yanked it up hard and threw her hip into the man's midsection. When he doubled over, she tripped him up and used his arm to flip him over. Between having her rear end grabbed and the man's back slamming into the floor, just two seconds had passed.

The blonde girl screamed and hopped up from her place astride the man. When she moved, Ava saw that the man's pants had been partially removed. When he reached for them, Ava drew her gun and pointed it at him.

"No one move," she said. She skirted her attention to the blond woman, currently attempting make a break for the door. "Not even you, sweetie."

"What the hell do you think you're doing?" the man on the floor cried out.

Ava placed her knee on his chest. "Who else is here?"

"No one! It's just us."

"You mean to tell me *you're* running this show? You opened the door for a woman you don't even know. Be real or I can make things very hard for you." She tapped his forehead with her gun and asked again. "Who else is here?"

"Floyd. He's in the back. But you can't go back there."

"I'll consider myself warned."

She withdrew her knee and started for the door on the right side of the room. When she heard the fallen man moving swiftly, she swiveled the gun back around on him.

"No, you can't go back there," the man said. "He'll kill you and then he'll beat me to a pulp."

"Listen to him," the pretty blonde woman said. "I've met Floyd. He's bad news. Just...I don't know why you're here, but you should go."

The look in the woman's eyes sent a flicker of fear through Ava but she carried on anyway. She opened the door and stepped into a dimly lit room. There were two beds, a single lamp, and nothing more. A man sat on the edge of one of the beds. A woman was under the sheets, crying.

The man was wearing a wide-brimmed hat, the sort some would call a fedora. When he saw Ava and her gun, he instantly made a run for it. Ava knew she couldn't shoot him. A cop shooting someone on a case that was not official was going to look very bad. Instead, she fired into the ceiling. It was effective enough, as the man instantly stopped and raised his hands into the air.

"Hey, it's not what it looks like," the man in the hat said. Standing in the lamplight, Ava saw that the man was of average height and a little overweight. In other words, this was not the man she was looking for—not the man who had killed Clarence. Still, there was something illicit going on here, and she couldn't just leave it be.

"Hands behind your head," Ava said.

The man did as asked. He moved slowly, as if he knew what to expect. As if he'd done this before. As Ava moved closer to him, she glanced to the crying woman on the bed. She was nude, holding a sheet against her body. She was bleeding from the lips and from a large cut over her right eye. Ava cringed when she took in the whole picture, realizing that there was no way this girl was any older than fifteen…sixteen at the most.

"Did he hurt you?" Ava asked the girl.

She nodded, hugging the sheet tighter. "I didn't mean to come here. They said they'd…said they'd help my dad pay for his house. We're so broke and…"

"It's okay," Ava said. She stepped closer to the man and had to restrain herself from clocking him in the back of the head. "What's your name?" she asked him.

"Floyd Lance."

"What did you do to this girl?"

He said nothing, likely because he couldn't bring himself to give it words. Ava weighed her options, realizing she'd painted herself into a bit of a corner here. She could not arrest them, as she wasn't on duty and was here because she was looking into Clarence's murder. But she had a name, at least. And a location.

"I'm leaving here with this girl," Ava said. "And if you know what's good for you, you'll get the hell out of here soon after that. And if I ever hear your name again, or even *think* you're doing this sort of thing, I'll find you."

"Oh yeah, you stupid dame?" Floyd said. He was trying to sound tough, but it was clear that he was scared. "And just who the hell are you, anyw—"

This time, Ava did hit him. She struck him in the back of the head with her gun—not the department-issued Smith and Wesson .38 but Clarence's old Colt. The sound was a bit gross, and he fell like a sack of rocks. Ava stared at him for a moment, alarmed that she'd done it with such ease.

She turned and reached out to the girl. "Can you walk?"

She nodded and took Ava's hand. Ava kept the girl close as they made their exit, bypassing the three people in the back room. She gave them no warnings, wanting to get the girl to safety in an anonymous fashion and then to get back home so she could figure out a believable story to get the department to look into a man named Floyd Lance. Maybe she could even figure out a way to talk someone into swinging by Clancy's one night at random.

It was going to be an interesting few days as she tried to knit it all together. But then again, every day had been both dangerous and interesting since she'd become a detective, so this was nothing new.

And to make matters even stranger, she had a dinner to get to.

He'll understand if I don't show up, she thought. *Even he thinks it's a bad idea.*

But as she ushered the young woman out of the back of Clancy's, she knew she was going to go. If they were going to work effectively together as partners, they needed to get this out of the way. They needed to put the understanding out there that this was a professional relationship and nothing more.

He was just going to have to deal with the fact that she was going to be a little late.

CHAPTER TWO

"You're late," Frank said.

"I know. I'm sorry. But I made it and I'm here now. So let's forget about the being-late thing."

"To be more specific, you're forty minutes late."

"Again, I'm sorry. I had some personal things I had to deal with."

"Do I want to know?"

She shrugged and hoped he'd leave it at that. After leaving the young girl on the steps of the post office two blocks from the precinct, she'd made an anonymous call from one of the city pay phones. She'd not left her place from behind the stoop of the bank one street over until she'd seen the cop car pulling up to speak with the girl. She then ran home, changed clothes, and walked to the small Italian restaurant Frank had chosen.

"I almost left, you know?" Frank said. They were sitting in the back of the restaurant, situated in a dark corner. Ava assumed this was intentional on Frank's part. One of the reasons they'd elected to meet at such a late hour was to make sure there were no prying eyes from the precinct. The corner table at the back of the place was an added precaution. It was very smart thinking.

"Why didn't you?" she asked.

"Because I tried to think the way you would. I know this is awkward and you're fighting your better judgment by being here, even though you were the one that asked *me* to dinner. So I asked myself how you'd think it out. I feel like I know you well enough by now. I figured you'd talk yourself out of it, then into it, then out of it again. The you'd decide to show up later—maybe half an hour to an hour— and tell yourself: *well, self, we tried, but he left when we were a little late.* And you'd tell yourself it was a sign and that we weren't supposed to have this dinner."

"That's some fine detective work."

"Am I right?"

"Maybe," she said, simply because it was much easier than trying to explain the truth. Already, even while sitting across from Frank, she was trying to come up with some convoluted explanation to get some attention on Floyd Lance as soon as possible.

"So, are we able to shoot straight with one another? We've been partners for about five weeks...almost six. That's enough time to stop pretending and just be honest, right?"

"Sure. What would you like me to be honest about?"

"I'd like you to be honest about how you feel about working with me. I want to know how you *really* feel about having all of this weight and pressure on you because you're a female detective in New York City."

It was odd, but Frank seemed to talk differently in a formal setting. His tone was a bit softer and the words came slower when he wasn't on a case. Ava found that she liked this version of Frank quite a bit.

"It's stressful but I'm trying not to see myself as any different than any other detectives."

"Do you find yourself comparing yourself to Clarence?"

"What do you mean?"

She could tell that he was choosing his words carefully, as mentioning Clarence was like treading on sacred ground. "I mean do you find yourself asking yourself what Clarence might do in any given situation?"

"Oh, for sure."

Before she could go deeper, the waiter brought their food. She noted that Frank said a very quick prayer to himself before he started eating—something she would never have expected out of him.

"So, I have a question," he said as he swirled some pasta around his fork. "Am I a total heartless bastard if I tell you that I have this...I don't know...this *feeling* about you?"

Ava knew the conversation would end up there eventually, but was surprised how quickly Frank had gotten to it. Then again, he'd been sitting on it for a few days, she supposed. This dinner was supposed to occur four days ago, and at her request following her little tantrum in front of the entire precinct, but she'd chickened out in the last moment. It had mostly been nerves but was also partly because she wasn't sure if she was ready to move on from the loss of Clarence.

"I guess it depends on the feeling."

"There's something there," he said quickly. "Between us, I mean. Something that feels like it could be more than a working relationship. I think you feel it, too."

"You do?"

11

"At the risk of sounding cocky, yes, I do. There are just little things here and there that I can't really put my finger on." He studied her for a moment and asked: "Am I totally wrong about that?"

"No, not *totally*," she said. And God, it hurt to say it. She started cutting into her Italian chicken, thinking of how to phrase it. "But I'll tell you right now that I'm not done truly grieving Clarence. Toss in this added pressure of the job *and* the fact that everyone is treating me like some deranged chick at work ever since I went off…"

"Yeah, that was nasty."

It had been. Ever since she'd made a scene and made her very vocal statement about how she would not be bullied, no one at the precinct would look at her. She could easily recall standing on Frank's desk and reading out the threatening letter than some other cop had sent to her. In doing so, she'd called out the entire department and no one aside from Frank seemed to be handling it well. Even Captain Minard had kept his distance in the four days between then and now.

"In other words," Ava said, "even if I was totally head over heels and ditzy for you, I couldn't do anything about it right now. There's just too much going on. It would be too messy."

Frank nodded in a way that told her he had expected this. Smiling, he looked at her and asked, "*Are* you any of those things for me?"

She smiled right back and said, "I think I'll keep that close to my chest for now."

The table fell into silence for a few minutes as they weighed all they'd just said and ate their dinner. She could tell there was something on Frank's mind and nearly asked him what he was thinking. Before she had the chance, he came out with it.

"Further down the road, if I try to pursue this…I know you have a son and a father. A father that is a very accomplished boxer, which scares me a bit. Do you think they would be open to you moving on with someone new?"

She'd honestly never even thought of it. She knew that Jeffrey hadn't truly processed the loss of his father and she even had some things to deal with if she wanted to truly let him go. As for her father, she didn't think he'd care one way or the other so long as she ended up with someone who treated her well.

"I honestly don't know," she answered. "But we can cross that bridge when we get there. Fair?"

"Fair enough. Only…what did we just decide?"

With a smirk, Ava said, "Nothing."

She did have to admit to herself, though, that the thought of going deeper with Frank was exciting. He was nice enough, polite even beyond his rough exterior. There was a ruggedness to him that made her feel safe, and he seemed to genuinely care about her. He was quite easy on the eyes, too, his well-defined chin almost daring someone to try to knock him down, while his dark hair and eyes seemed both impenetrable and inviting a challenge all at once.

But even thinking of him in that way felt like a betrayal of Clarence. And for now, that was the only answer she needed.

So they left it at that, moving the conversation on to work matters. Yet, the entire time they spoke, Ava's mind was elsewhere. She saw that young girl in the bed, she saw Floyd Lance from behind—a man she'd been hoping would turn out to be the man who had killed her husband. She'd left loose ends everywhere and if she wasn't careful, she knew this private quest to find Clarence's killer may very well destroy everything she'd worked for.

***

When she returned home, Ava found herself pausing by the door to her apartment before unlocking it. It was nearing eleven o'clock, and she had no idea if her father would still be awake. More than that, though, she'd been hesitating outside the door for the past few days, still haunted by the afternoon when she'd come home and found the dead rat and a threatening note left behind by the mob. Of course, the mob had not actually claimed the grisly gifts, but Ava knew.

Finally unlocking the door, she stepped inside and found the place completely quiet. All the lights were out and the curtains had been drawn. She looked over to the window she'd had replaced after someone had broken in—also very likely the mob as far as she was concerned. Thinking back on it all, it made her think twice about her sudden idea to use Tony Two's name tonight.

As she quietly made her way into the bathroom to get ready for bed, she thought very briefly of August Bonnaci, the mobster capo who had vowed to help find out who had been hard on her. She wondered if he was being true to his word and if so, what he might be doing. All Ava knew for certain was ever since the window had been broken and someone had entered her apartment a couple of days ago, nothing else had happened. So apparently, Bonnaci was doing *something* behind the scenes. She thought about paying him a visit in the back room of his restaurant but figured that would be a bad idea. August Bonnaci, like most effective mobsters, did their in-work with cops in the shadows. Sure, it was a well-known fact that the two often went hand in hand, but neither side worked to broadcast it.

Before heading to bed, she looked back into the living room where her father, Roosevelt Burr, was snoring softly on the couch. She then checked in on Jeffrey, who was also fast asleep. She place her hand on his chest, said a quick prayer for him, and headed to bed. When she lay down, she found that some of the adrenaline from the action at Clancy's was still pummeling through her and her mind was also busy trying to decipher what her dinner with Frank might mean. It took her forever to fall asleep but when she finally did, the last image her mind conjured was of the last night Clarence had been here with her, in the bed, taking up the other side. She reached out to a man who was not there as sleep finally pulled her under.

CHAPTER THREE

When she entered the precinct the following morning, Ava felt like she was walking through a museum. The people she passed by seemed motionless, like odd displays. Some went out of their way not to look at her and others stared her down as if hoping they could cause her to spontaneously burst into flame. Who knew that a woman speaking her mind would cause so many people to get sore. Ignoring the cold shoulders and stares, she headed downstairs to where the offices for the Women's Bureau were located. There'd been a bit more talk around the office about the WB ever since Ava had been promoted to detective and she was quite proud of that. Some of the women down there—France and Lottie, in particular—deserved the same shot she'd been given.

She was a bit surprised to find Frank down in the WB when she passed through the doors. When he turned to greet her, she noticed that Frances and Lottie were giving her amused smiles behind Frank's back. There were a few other ladies at their desks, but none of them paid Ava much mind. She often wondered if there was some resentment from some of the other women, of how she'd been practically handed the role of detective. It was one of the reasons she strived so hard to do the job well.

"Fancy meeting you here," Ava said.

"I got here early and figured this was the first place you'd come."

"Okay, sure…but why are you here?"

Lottie cackled and said, "Isn't it obvious? He can't stand to be away from me. This outfit *does* show off these gams, don't you think?" She outstretched her perfect leg, though she was being sarcastic; the outfits the WB were made to wear did absolutely nothing to flatter their female figure—and with good reason, as far as Ava was concerned.

"Lottie's daydreams aside," Frank said, "I wanted to make sure I saw you down here before I saw you upstairs. The moment I got in this morning, Minard asked if you were in yet. When I told him I didn't think so, he told me that the moment you got in, he needed to speak with us. I figured it would be better to tell you here, among friends, rather than upstairs."

"Upstairs," Ava said, "where I *have* no friends."

"Well…where people are going to stare and assume things the moment they see you and I walk into Minard's office together. So I'm going to head up now, and I figure you can trail behind me in about two or three minutes."

"Seems sort of juvenile, but yes…let's do it like that."

Frank gave her a nod and then looked out to the other women in the room. "Ladies," he said in a dashing manner, and then made his exit.

"Damn," Lottie said. "I don't know how you work alongside him like you do. I would eat that mac alive."

"That's charming, Lottie."

"Aww, sweetie, if you think men come after me for my charm, I think there's a thing or two I need to teach you."

"Zip it, Lottie," Frances said, walking over to Ava. "You okay? I know it's been tough the last few days."

"Yeah, I'm fine. Same old, same old, you know? Just a world full of men that get really scared and uncomfortable when a woman dares to speak loudly."

"Well then, you lead the way for us," Frances said with a grin.

It was an encouraging idea, but Ava could not shake the nerves as she left the WB office and started up the stairs. As soon as she stepped back onto the first floor, she felt like all eyes and thoughts were on her. She knew it was a little vain to feel such a way, but the iciness of the room toward her could not be denied. She headed straight for Minard's office, where she knocked on the door and was called in right away. It was odd to realize that she felt a little less awkward in Minard's office. The icy stares were gone and Minard had started showing her a bit more respect over the past few weeks.

Minard looked slightly flustered but not quite angry. His dark, clumpy hair—which was starting to thin out at the top—was combed nicely and he was clean-shaven. It made Ava think he'd had a morning free of rushing and stress, giving him enough time to actually make sure he looked good when he left the house. In a strange way, it made it hard for her to read him.

Frank stood in the corner, occupying himself by looking at the spines of some of the larger books on Minard's cluttered bookshelf.

"Go on and have a seat," Minard told her.

That told her what she needed to know. Had he *ever* told her to take a seat? It made her wonder what sort of bad news he was about to drop on her. She sat down, looking at Frank to see if his face gave anything away. But it seemed he was just as clueless as she was.

"I find myself in a bit of a bad situation," Minard said. "Gold, it's no secret that your little display while standing on top of Wimbly's desk has alienated you. I've gotten countless complaints from other officers, worried that you're getting too big for your britches. Others feel slighted that you were given the promotion to detective so quickly, and they think it's gone to your head."

"But sir, I—"

He held up a hand to silence her. "So for the past few days, I've been trying to figure out some way to make sure everyone is happy—so my other officers and detectives will stop bumping gums about you, but also trying to keep you busy. Because whether they all like it or not, the truth of the matter remains that you have been a godsend for this precinct when it comes to the media. The story pretty much writes itself. We're being painted in a positive light, which is a huge plus when compared to stories of dirty cops working with the mob."

He stopped here and took a deep breath. The pause went on so long that Ava wondered if she should say something. Instead, Minard pushed a single sheet of paper over to her.

"Then this morning, I got this over the wire. There's a case in Brooklyn that they could use a homicide detective on. I want you to take it."

"Of course," she said, taking the report. "I feel like I'm missing something, though. You seem…flustered."

"It's more than just taking the case," he explained. "You'll be working out of the 77th precinct for a few days."

"So I'm being relocated because a few men raised hell about me?"

"You're being relocated because this precinct needs an extra homicide detective," he said, raising his voice. "The basics are there, in the report. A female reporter was killed while looking into a story. Rumors suggest it might have been related to mob activity. It's an amazing opportunity for all of us. It will get you out of here for a few days and let tempers die down. And it helps *you* because it'll give another part of the city the chance to cheer you on. It'll help spread your story."

"Which would continue to help *this* precinct look good," Frank said, catching on. He said it in a monotone way, making Ava assume he was not a fan of it.

"What about Detective Wimbly?" Ava asked. "Will he be coming as well?"

"No. This will just be you. I imagine they might partner you up with someone else on their end."

The amount of despair she felt over this alarmed her and told her more about how she was truly starting to feel about Frank than their dinner had the night before. She saw the look of shock in Frank's face, too, though he hid it right away. Looking back to Minard, she saw there was no point in refusing the job. Besides, all of the reasons he'd given made perfect sense, as much as she didn't agree with some of it.

"And when am I supposed to start?" she asked.

"Right away. Take a cab as soon as you can. They're expecting you."

She took up the report, realizing that she hadn't even read it yet. "Yes, sir." She glanced tentatively at Frank as she opened the door She had nearly stepped through when another thought hit her.

"Captain? I'm curious…I heard a lady down in the WB talking about a young girl that was found last night, right up the street. Is that true?"

"I suppose so. There was a brief report on my desk. She's been taken to an orphanage." He eyed her suspiciously and said: "Why do you ask?"

The lie came a little too easily for her own comfort. She shrugged and said, "I see them sometimes on the street and it breaks my heart. There are far too many discarded kids in this city." Then, wanting to bounce back from her ruse as quickly as possible, she flashed the one-page report up. "I'll head right over."

As she pulled the door closed behind her, she noticed that neither man looked particularly happy that she was going, but then again, neither of them made any argument for her to stay.

***

She walked the several blocks between the precinct to her father's gym. Being that it was nearing nine in the morning, the place was dead; the men who came in for early morning sessions were long gone and no one else was likely to show up until well after lunch. She found her father replacing the padding on one of the posts to the primary boxing ring. He looked surprised to see her but didn't look away from his work.

"I haven't done anything illegal, I swear!" he joked with her as she approached the ring apron.

"Even if you had, I'd let you slide." She leaned against the ring and stared at him through the ropes. It was so easy to recall the sessions she'd enjoyed in this very same ring. They'd usually been against her dad, but a few younger men had also taken on the challenge. She knew they'd initially taken it easy on her, but had learned their lesson the hard way. In the silence of the empty gym, she realized just how much she missed slipping a pair of gloves on and sparring. It had been far too long—two years at least.

"Dad, I know it's becoming a pretty common thing as of late, but I need to ask a favor."

"You need me to pick Jeffrey up from school."

"Yeah, good guess."

"Ava, you know I don't mind doing it."

"I know. But I had fully planned on doing it today. And I hate to assume you're just okay with it. I've got this case out in Brooklyn I'm headed to and I don't know what it's going to look like. I have no idea at all when I'll be home."

She hated that her new job was making her feel inconsistent. More than that, it was making her feel like an awful mother. Apparently, it showed in her expression.

"Don't," Roosevelt said. "Jeffrey thinks you're like a superhero, you know? You keep doing your job, and I'll keep helping take care of him." He grinned and got to his feet, checking his work on the padding. "Believe it or not, I'm not too bad at it."

"I know you're not. Thanks, Dad." She stepped up on the side of the ring and, with the ropes between them, gave him a hug.

She hopped down and was halfway back across the floor toward the door when he called out after her. "Hey, Ava?"

She turned and saw him looking down at her, leaning on the ropes. For a moment she saw him as she had when she'd been a little girl, swaying on the ropes in exhaustion after a match. "Yes, sir?"

"I noticed you got in late last night. I know you're capable of handling yourself, but...it makes me wonder if you might be getting into things outside of your work that you shouldn't be sniffing around."

She appreciated the comment and concern, but said nothing. She was afraid that if she did, they'd get into a whole conversation about it—about how she was spending a lot of her free time looking for

Clarence's killer. And with the way this morning had already gone, that was not something she wanted to get into.

"I'm fine, Dad," she said with a wink. "I promise."

With that, she left the gym and stepped out to the curb where she started looking for a cab that would take her to Brooklyn.

CHAPTER FOUR

When Ava stepped into the 77th precinct in Brooklyn twenty-five minutes later, she imagined she could hear a pin drop. The first person to notice her was a policeman who had just come in through the front doors. He nudged an officer beside him, and so on. By the time this not-so-subtle nudging was done, a woman sitting at a dank reception desk had seen her and was spreading the word to the bullpen area behind her.

It took all of twenty seconds for it to feel like the first day at her home precinct all over again. With no clear direction where to go, she headed to the nosy nellies at the reception desk. The woman she chose to walk directly toward sat straight up and did her best to look extra-professional.

"I'm Ava Gold, sent over from the 54th Precinct. Is the Chief currently in?"

"He is, and he's been expecting you. Go around the dick's section, hit the hallway, and Chief Skinner's office is the first one on the left." The woman smiled the entire time she spoke and Ava got the feeling that it was genuine.

She followed the directions she'd been given and the catcalls started almost right away. She heard a very high-pitched whistling, and a singular *"Yow!"* Someone even blurted out: "You need someone to show you around, sweet thing?" A series of boyish snickers followed this.

She didn't bother turning to find the sources, as she didn't want to give them the attention. Again, she felt as if she'd stepped back in time and was starting all over again. She could feel her cheeks growing red as she pushed down about a hundred possible retorts and comebacks. Instead, she kept her head down and made her way to the hallway. When she knocked on the door of Chief Skinner's office, the laughing and hooting stopped.

"Come on in," came a loud, boisterous voice.

Ava opened the door and stepped inside to find a very large man sitting behind a desk that looked to be cluttered with several years' worth of paperwork. The polite way to describe Captain Skinner was

21

rotund. He was extremely overweight and when he smiled at her, his cheeks looked more like jowls. He did not bother getting to his feet but he did extend a single pudgy hand across his desk.

"Detective Gold?" he asked.

"Yes, sir. I came over as quickly as I could." She shook the offered hand and found it plump and sweaty.

"Well, I'm Captain Skinner. I'm glad you were available to come help out."

"Of course. I understand there's a homicide case you need assistance with?"

"A homicide c—" He stared. He seemed confused for a moment and did a very bad job of hiding it when he picked his stream of thought back up. "Yes, yes, the homicide case. There was a journalist shot in the street yesterday—a woman. I've had two of my men on it but they haven't found anything yet. Because it's a woman reporter and she was capped pretty close to a rough part of town, I think you'd be a good fit."

Ava was fairly certain he was lying. About what, she wasn't quite sure. But she did have the report and there was a murder to solve. She decided to keep her questions about Skinner's confusion to herself for now.

"Could I see the existing reports your men put together?"

"Of course, of course," he said. He moved as quickly as he could through one of the stacks of files and papers on his desk. After about twenty seconds, he pulled out a single folder. It contained three sheets of paper inside and the notes were extremely sparse.

"This is it?"

"Yes, they weren't able to find much."

"And you just want me to take a crack at it?"

"Yes, of course," he said. He was speaking very quickly and his eyes had a shifty quality to them. It was quite evident that he wanted her out of his hair as soon as possible. It made no sense to her at first but then she replayed the conversation with Minard in his office. He'd seemed a bit off as well. Slowly, it dawned on her that this precinct had not reached out to Minard at all. No, this was the Brooklyn precinct doing Minard a favor; she was willing to bet just about anything that Minard had called for a favor just to get her out of their precinct for a while.

She gripped the insignificantly thin folder tightly, knowing that even asking such a thing to Skinner would open up a mess. More than that, she found that she was actually a little upset with herself. Had she really already started to think so much of herself that she assumed another precinct *would* be clamoring to get her help?

"I'm on it, then," she said. "Thanks."

She left quickly, glad to leave Skinner behind. Yet, of course, the moment she was back in the larger part of the building and circling around the bullpen, there were more catcalls and whistling. She heard someone make a whispered comment about her breasts. But she kept her head down, determined to make it out of the building without flipping her wig on someone.

She nearly made it back to the reception desk when her path was blocked. A man in a suit, the suit making her assume he was a detective or some other form of gumshoe, stood directly in her path. He was middle-aged and his face was downturned into a scowl that somehow made him look older.

"You got that dead journalist case?" he asked.

"Seems like it."

He chuckled and took a step closer to her. He smelled like donuts and cigarette smoke when he leaned in close and said, "Good luck with that, you simple jane. That was my case, and my partner and I didn't find a damn thing. Maybe when you come up empty-handed you can swing back by here and make us all a nice, warm dinner."

Ava glared at him for only a moment before she kept walking forward. She pushed past him, to the sound of more laughter from behind her. It made her wish Frank was there or, more to the point, that Minard had not seen fit to send her off on this pointless errand just to appease the coppers back at her precinct. It felt far too similar to her first few days on the job and she was not prepared to handle all of that again.

To hell with it, she thought. With the small report in hand, she figured the best form of revenge she could get on the snickering morons behind her *and* on Minard would be to solve the case. So that's exactly what she planned to do.

CHAPTER FIVE

There was a bench directly in front of the precinct, but Ava passed it by. She wanted to get as far away from the leering and insulting men as she could. She opted for a bench two blocks over, situated between an apartment building and a deli. There, she opened up the file and looked over its very brief contents.

Early yesterday afternoon, an up-and-coming female journalist by the name of Millie Newsom had been shot and killed in broad daylight. There were upwards of eight witnesses who claimed to have heard the shot and then watched Millie fall, but no one had seen the shooter. By the time the police arrived, any potential shooter on the scene would have had a twenty-minute head start. No one had noticed anyone fleeing the scene. No clues, no help, nothing.

Other than the location and the name of the coroner that received the body, the report offered little else. Ava weighed her options, already aware that this was the sort of case that was stacked against her. No eyewitnesses who saw the shooter and so close to a side of town that was seen by most to be seedy.

Noting that the body had arrived at the coroner's late last night, she wondered if they'd be able to offer anything of note. Figuring it was as good a starting place as any, she got to her feet and hailed a cab. An older jalopy pulled to the sidewalk within a minute and she was on her way—realizing that it was the first official case she'd be running solo.

As she watched the somewhat unfamiliar streets of Brooklyn pass by, she couldn't help but wonder what Frank thought about this situation. More than that, she wondered if he'd known it was coming. Captain Minard seemed to respect him more and not just because they were both men. Frank had several years more experience than she did, and Ava also understood that she was something of a controversial figure. But she found it hard to believe Minard would just drop something like this on Frank. But she also recalled their dinner from the night before; Frank had seemed genuine and almost vulnerable. To think he'd keep a secret like this from her seemed unlikely.

They're trying to see if you'll just give up. It was Clarence's voice in her head, one she'd been hearing less and less over the past few days. The comment made no sense at first, but then she figured it out. Sure, Minard talked about how her image was good for the precinct and how she was becoming something of a public figure. Given that, why would he and other men like him want her to fail?

Simple: because her failure would be a public one. It would be Exhibit A in how women just weren't cut out for this kind of work.

She was deep into this thinking when the cab came to a stop. She'd been so caught up in her own thoughts that she didn't realize they'd reached the coroner's office. It was a simple office that looked quite plain from the outside. She would have never guessed the coroner's office was inside, other than the fact that the hospital was just two blocks away.

She paid the cabbie and got out. When she walked into the office, she did her best to make it appear as if she made visits like this all the time. She walked directly to the front desk where she was greeted by an older man smoking a pipe.

"Help you?" he asked, the pipe still clenched between his back teeth.

Ava showed her ID. "I'm Detective Ava Gold from the 54th Precinct in Manhattan. I need to speak to the coroner about a body that came in yesterday."

"Detective?" he said, shocked. He then leaned in closer and eyed her ID as if he were inspecting a piece of questionable fruit. Fragrant pipe smoke wafted up into her face. Finally, he said, "Huh. Well, Tuck is in the back. Knock before you go in, though. You never know what he's in the middle of."

Ava did not like the grin the old man flashed her way, broke by the pipe reed. She stepped around the front desk and headed down a hallway that, to her, felt and smelled exactly like the hallway of a hospital. She passed a few doors until arriving at the large one at the end of the hall with the glass partition near the top that read CORONER right across the center. Taking the pipe-smoking gentleman's advice, she knocked and waited.

She got a response right away. It was surprisingly cheerful, considering where it was coming from. "Come on in!"

She opened the door and was rather relieved to find that the examination table that took up the center of the room was empty. A tall, thin man with slicked back black hair stood by a long back counter, filling out paperwork. He looked up at Ava and smiled curiously.

"Um, can I help you?" he asked.

She again showed her ID (something she was beginning to enjoy) and introduced herself. "Detective Ava Gold, out of Manhattan. I was sent in to help the 77th Precinct with a murder that occurred yesterday. A female reporter who was shot."

"Yes," he said, a bit too cheerfully. "Millie Newsom. Do you need to see the body?"

Ava honestly had no idea if that was necessary but she wanted to seem as natural as possible, so the first words out of her mouth were: "Yes, please."

"This way. I just finished with her last night. You're just in time; I believe she'd headed to the funeral director later today."

He led her to the back of the large room, where there was a heavy metal door. It had a latch opening—the sort she'd often seen butchers go into when they had to go to the back of their store to get choice cuts of meat. He walked in, flicking on an electric light as he did so. The room beyond the metal door was illuminated in a harsh glow and what Ava saw made her freeze up, despite her attempt at looking natural.

First of all, the room was very cold. She spotted the refrigeration unit in the back, chugging along with the noise of a very confused beast. Secondly, the room was filled with what looked to be slab-like cots on wheels. There were twenty of them, and thirteen were occupied. Each body was covered with a white sheet that looked almost impossibly clean.

"Here we go," the coroner said as he weaved through one of the rows. He came to the second cot on the second row, checked a small handwritten tag on the body's toe, and nodded. Pulling back the sheet, he said: "Millie Newson, age twenty-eight, died of a gunshot wound. I know the killer has not yet been caught, but the reason for death is a pretty simple one. The gunshot entered through her back and passed upward through her, at an angle. The bullet pierced her heart and got lodged in her breastbone."

Ava looked at the woman, taking it in. She'd seen several dead bodies before, but in all but one case, it had been in the confines of a funeral home or church. She saw the work the coroner had done along her chest, just above her left breast. Ava felt immense sorrow for the woman. She'd been young and very pretty, with her entire life in front of her. Why kill her? Was it because she'd been a woman in a job market traditionally run by men? Had she maybe made some enemies somewhere along the line while doing research for her articles? It made

Ava angry as well as sad, and she could feel both emotions swirling inside of her.

"Do you happen to still have the bullet?" she asked.

"I do!" He looked down at Millie Newsom's body and said, "Are we done here?"

"Yes. Thank you."

He covered the body back up and led Ava back into the primary examination room. He went to the large counter in the back and opened one of several drawers. He plucked a small envelope out right away and handed it over to her.

"Seems like a pretty common type," he told her as Ava dumped the slug out into her palm. "I've seen a lot of these over the last few years. Small caliber, from a handgun. Most likely a revolver."

Ava nodded, glad that he was bumping his gums endlessly because she had yet to learn much about guns. She sure as hell wouldn't be able to match a fired round with the gun it had come from, that was for sure. Not that it mattered—not right now, anyway. The bit of information her brain was hung up on was the fact that she'd been shot from behind. It seemed like a very cowardly act and surely someone would have seen something like that, right?

There was no way to answer that while standing in the coroner's office. She slipped the spent bullet back into the envelope and handed it to the coroner. "Thanks for your time."

"Of course. And good luck out there!"

Ava headed back outside, passing by the smell of pipe smoke from the front desk. On the street, she once again hailed a cab, only this time she was headed to the scene of the crime to get a better look at the last place Millie Newsom had been seen alive.

***

The crime scene was closer to the precinct than Ava would have thought—no more than a mile and a half at most. Millie had been shot on a little side street with a gradual downhill slope to it. It wasn't what Ava would have referred to as "the bad part of town," but it did seem to be a thoroughfare that connected the more reputable part of Brooklyn with the seedier areas.

She canvassed the area for less than thirty seconds before she saw the smudged chalk lines the police had drawn on the sidewalk to show where the body had fallen. There was also a very faded splotch within the shape and just outside of it. Blood splatter that had been cleaned up afterwards no doubt.

To Ava, the most disconcerting part of it all was that people had been walking over the outline all morning, to the point where it had nearly been rubbed away—as if a woman had not been murdered here less that twenty-four hours ago. She stood in the center of what remained of the chalk outline and surveyed the street from that perspective. From the shape of the outline, Ava thought it was a safe bet to assume that Millie had been walking *down* the street.

To her immediate right, there was the street. It was currently empty of traffic but there were two automobiles further down that were headed in her direction. To her left, there were two buildings. One looked to be a down-on-its-luck furrier and the other was a basic department store. A bit further up the street, back toward the better part of town, she saw a newsstand. A lone man stood behind it, wearing respectable clothes and a stylish driver's cap. He nodded politely to her as she approached him.

She showed her ID (it really never did get old) and gave her name. "I'm looking into the case of the woman who was shot here yesterday. Were you standing right here when it happened?"

"Aye, I was," the newsie said in a slight Irish accent. "But I was talking to a customer and looking out this way when it happened." He hitched a thumb behind him, back toward the main street that sat slightly uphill. "By the time I turned around from the shot, I was ducking for protection and the lady was already on the street."

"And you saw no one that would have maybe been the shooter?"

"Sure didn't."

Ava looked from the newsstand to the chalk outline. She suspected from the fact that there were no witnesses at all, Millie had likely not been shot by someone else standing on the street. She looked up but saw no second-floor terraces. There was only a single window over the furrier's shop but the look of it alone told her it was old and had likely not been touched in a very long time. Not that it really mattered, though; the coroner had explained the angle as having come at an upward angle, meaning the shot would not have come from up high.

Ava walked down the street a bit, looking for alleyways. She saw only one, separating the furrier from a small discount store. She stepped into it and looked toward the chalk outline. The shot could have certainly been pulled off from there, but the alley dead-ended about fifty yards away in a sturdy wooden fence. Had the killer shot from here, he would have had to either be trapped by the fence or rush out into the street. But none of the eyewitnesses had noted anything like that.

In other words, there just wasn't enough to go on. For all she knew the killer could have been riding by in a car. If the car was loud enough, it could have even covered up the sound of the gunshot for those standing close enough to it.

With no answers down that stream of thought, Ava tried another. She had Millie Newsom's home address in the report Skinner had given her, and it was nowhere near where she currently stood. She assumed this meant Millie had been headed somewhere for whatever story she had been working on. And if it *was* centered around a story, was there someone involved in it who had taken it upon themselves to kill her?

Had Millie been following someone who simply didn't want to be followed? For a shooter to be hidden so well or to be so accurate with a gun and so stealthy afterwards, Ava thought there was a good chance this was the case. She also knew there was only one place she could go in order to find out.

CHAPTER SIX

The offices of *The Brooklyn Eagle* were located on Old Fulton Street, an area of the city Ava was wholly unfamiliar with. When she stepped in through the front doors, it was a bit crazier than she'd expected. A flurry of different conversations hit her the moment she walked in. The musical click-clacking of numerous typewriters filled the air, and she saw two people running quickly between desks, carrying sheets of paper. She was amazed and amused that the offices of a daily newspaper were busier and more high energy that any police department she'd ever seen.

There was a small desk just off the front door, but no one was sitting at it. Ava stepped into the large open area that served as the hub of the building. She heard the ringing of a phone somewhere in the distance and someone in the background shouting for someone else to get them those damned sports scores.

Sensing that she could quickly get lost in the hectic pace of the place, Ava reached out and grabbed the arm of the first person who passed by her. It was a middle-aged man wearing bifocals and he looked to be in an enormous hurry.

"Sorry to interrupt you," she said. "I need to speak to whoever is in charge."

"That's going to be Albert Palmer, the senior editor. But unless you have an appointment, I doubt he'll have the time."

"Where would I find him?"

Clearly irritated that he was being delayed to wherever he was headed, the man pointed to the back wall located behind the clamoring madness. She saw several doors and two windows looking out from offices spaces onto the work floor. "Last door on the right."

With that, the man resumed his rush, hurrying to a desk on the other side of the room. Ava made her way carefully across the room, through the sounds of the typewriter and hurried voices. The odd thing was, though, that they all seemed to thoroughly enjoy their job. There was excitement and purpose in their hurried pace as they raced to get the news ready for the following day.

She came to the back of the room and knocked on the door she'd been directed to. For the third time in under three hours, a man yelled from the other side. "What is it?"

It wasn't an invitation to come in, but Ava opened the door anyway. Inside, there was a man sitting behind a large desk. There was a typewriter, several pens, and a cup of coffee sitting on the right side of the desk. The left side was covered in stacks of paper. There were five in all, not including the few sheets that sat right in front of the man. He glanced up at her from those papers, a pen gripped in his hand.

"Who're you?"

She reached for her ID again but before she had a chance to properly show it, the editor—presumably Albert Palmer—stopped her.

"Wait a second! I know who you are! Ava Gold, right?"

"That's right," she said. "How did you know?"

"I know because I'm the senior editor at this paper. And any newspaper editor in this city knows your face and name. Whether you know it or not, you're starting to make some small headlines."

"That's what I hear. Mr. Palmer, I see that you're very busy, but I was wondering if I could have just a few minutes of your time. I've been sent out here to look into the death of one of your reporters."

"Millie..." he said. In just speaking her name, his voice was thick with emotion.

"Yes, Millie Newsom. What can you tell me about her? Did you know what she was doing in that part of town yesterday?"

"Ah, well, Millie was always on the go, but only for work. She had no husband, and no suitor that I know of. Much like you, she was determined to show the world that women are just as capable—if not more so—than men. Another two years or so and she would have been at the top."

"So she was a good employee?"

"Oh, for sure. A great writer, a great interviewer, and always delivered clean copy. She was a great source for ideas, too."

"Was it a story that took her out to that side of town yesterday?"

"You know, I just don't know. She was in between stories, sort of just writing whatever I sent her way. Small things, what we call fluff pieces. She'd written a piece yesterday morning about the World's Fair. Handed it in and said she was taking the rest of the day off."

"Do you think she could have been digging into a story she had an idea for and maybe hadn't presented to you yet?"

When he didn't answer right away, Ava looked into his face. He looked worried about something, his brow furrowed. When he finally answered, he looked back down to the story he was currently editing.

"If that's what she was doing, I had no knowledge about it."

She felt like he was being dishonest—maybe not telling her an outright lie, but not being fully truthful.

"And you're sure there was nothing she was actively working on?"

"Detective Gold, Millie Newsom was one of my very best journalists. If she was working on a story, I assure you I would have known about it."

Ava nodded, sensing that Palmer was quickly getting tired of her intrusion. And if he truly *was* being dishonest, she knew that frustration would only grow. So she asked only one more question, thinking it might offer just a bit more insight into not only Millie Newsom's character, but why she might have been in that area of the city.

"Was Millie the sort that would take risks to get to the bottom of a story? That is, were you surprised to find that she was killed there?"

"I'm usually very aware of where I send my journalists. But Millie…she was fearless for sure. I don't know why she was there in that part of town, but I'm sure she had a good reason."

"Does she have a desk here?"

"She does. It's at the end of the hallway just to the side of my office."

"Would you allow me to have a look around it?"

"Of course," he said, but his face seemed to say otherwise. "But I had a look myself this morning. The cops that came through yesterday left it in one big mess."

"Did they find anything?"

"If they did, they didn't tell me."

"Thank you," she said, turning to leave. She glanced back and saw that Palmer had gone right back to his work before she'd even closed the door.

She looked to the right and saw the hallway he'd been talking about. It was short, containing only the restrooms, a secondary room for coffee and breaks, and then a small office space at the back. The door was open but she still knocked on it before entering.

"Yes?" a woman's voice said.

Ava stepped inside and found three desks, all pushed together to create a crude little workspace. A woman sat behind one of them, an older woman with graying hair. When she looked up at Ava, she looked tired and sad. She supposed the desk that looked like a tornado had hit it was Millie's—and if so, she'd sat directly across from this woman.

"I'm Detective Ava Gold," she said. "Mr. Palmer gave me permission to have a look at Millie's desk."

"Good luck with it," the woman said. "The cops that came in yesterday evening already tore through it."

"Were you here when they did it?"

"Yes. They weren't rude or anything, but they weren't much in the way of making sure they kept things neat, as you can see."

This was an understatement. Papers were scattered everywhere and in no discernable order. As she thumbed through them, she saw it was mostly handwritten notes, despite the clunky old typewriter sitting on the desk. Thinking of Millie Newsom and this older lady back here gave her the same feel as the WB office back in Manhattan. She guessed the female reporters had been stuck back here as an afterthought.

"Ma'am, do you happen to know if Millie was working on any current stories?"

"I'm not sure. But if she was, I'd know. She always bounced ideas off of me. And my God, she would not shut up when she had a story that was going well."

"She really liked her job, huh?"

"Oh, yes."

Ava studied the handwritten notes and even a few drafts of articles that had apparently gone nowhere: a piece on a new restaurant, a new pick-up baseball league coming to town, and a pianist coming from London to play a concert. As for the notes, they were mostly unreadable, scrawled in the sort of handwriting only the writer could read. She doubted they were of any importance because they were mostly just one- and two-word notes with little question marks beside them.

When she was certain there was nothing important there, Ava stepped back, imagining a pair of cops tearing through Millie's belongings. Surely something would have fallen on the floor, right? She dropped down to her hands and knees, but all she saw under her desk were a few little dust balls. On the way back up to her feet, though, she saw something at the very last second. It was so brief, she thought she'd imagined it.

Ava went back to her knees and craned her neck into the cutaway section in the center of the desk made for leg space. She then looked up and saw that her eyes had not deceived her after all. There was a small piece of paper taped to the underside of the desk. She used her fingernails to dig under the tape, pulling the piece of paper free.

When she got back to her feet, the older woman at the next desk was looking at her with great interest. "Find something?"

Ava looked at the paper. There was a name and an address written on it: *George Spotnitz, 551 Holloway Street.*

"Ma'am, do you happen to know a man named George Spotnitz?"

The woman gave a thin smile and shrugged. "It doesn't ring any bells, but that really doesn't mean much in this job. I could have easily spoken to someone with that name recently and just can't recall."

"Would you happen to know where Millie was headed yesterday when she left here?"

"I don't. Sorry. But you know...there *is* someone who might be able to help you. Millie had a young man working with her—sort of an apprentice that was trailing her. I don't know if he was with her yesterday, but maybe he could answer some of your questions."

Ava found this strange, as there had been no mention of this person in the police reports, and Captain Skinner hadn't mentioned him. "Is he here today?"

"I don't think so. I haven't seen him. He was more of a part-time employee. Still in training and all."

An apprentice who followed Millie Newsom around who just happened to not be here on the day after she was killed. That was just a little too coincidental as far as Ava was concerned. "What's his name?"

"Ronald Amberley," the older lady said as she started looking through a small stack of papers on her desk. "And here's his address." She copied it down onto a scrap piece of paper from one of the sheets on her desk. "I'm sure he'd love to find who did this. He really looked up to her."

"Thank you." Ava took the offered address and put it, along with the name and address she'd found under Millie's desk, into her pocket.

She left the office and thought about paying Skinner another visit to see why he'd neglected to tell her about the apprentice, Ronald Amberley. But rather than waste her time with dishonesty, she thought it might be better to just go find out herself.

CHAPTER SEVEN

Ronald Amberley lived in a small apartment building several blocks away from the precinct. It was a small, one-story building that looked to only hold about a dozen or so apartments within the interior. When Ava approached Amberley's door and knocked, she made a point to keep her head close to the door. His absence from work already had Ava suspicious of him—and the fact that Skinner had not mentioned him wasn't helping either. So, following her knock, she made sure to listen closely for any sounds of subtle movement from inside just in case he was indeed home, but opting not to answer the door.

Twenty seconds passed without any answer, so she knocked again. Still, no one answered the door.

Ava weighed her options, knowing she didn't have many. She did have one idea and the fact that this was only a one-story building was going to play in her favor. She hurried back outside and walked around the side of the building. There were no windows along the side, but the back had several. The back of the building looked out onto a small side street and, on the other side of that street, a row of nameless buildings that looked to all be in some stage of construction. She made sure that she was following the layout of the building correctly, counting the windows in relation to where Amberley's apartment was located.

She walked up to the window and peeked inside. She found herself looking into a small living area, occupied by only a couch and a very small coffee table. There were scattered sheets of paper on the table and the floor, but that was all she could see. She placed her hands along the edge of the windows and pushed up but it would not budge. She toyed with the idea of breaking the glass but even she knew that was a bit too much in order to get a good look at the apartment of someone who was barely a suspect.

On the other hand, she convinced herself that if she could find some way to get inside without breaking anything, that might be okay. And while that also an ill-advised idea, she knew she needed to solve this case. It was no longer simply about proving a point for herself; after seeing Millie Newsom's office and feeling the similarities between how she'd been treated with her own work situation, she felt a sort of kinship with the dead journalist.

But how far was she willing to go? Would she really break into an apartment, even when she had no real evidence against the man who lived there?

"Yes," she said to herself. "Yes, I would."

She headed back inside and once again approached Amberley's door. A thought had occurred to her—a memory, really—of a time one of the drummers she'd once worked with had accidentally locked their tuning key in the dressing room. With only five minutes left before showtime and no one in the venue to unlock the door, Ava had watched as a singer from another band had rushed to the door, teasing a hairpin out of her well-coiffed hair. She'd picked the lock with the hairpin, impressing everyone standing around the scene, including Ava.

Ava's hair was done very simply, some of the length pulled up and pinned in place to keep it off of her lower back. She reached up and removed one of the metal pins and then did her best to recall the way that singer had bent the top of it. It had not been at a straight, vertical angle but almost a ninety-degree angle. When she thought she had it right, she pressed down on what she'd bent and slid the pressed-together pin into the lock along the knob. She had to shove it a bit but when it finally did slide in, it went rather smoothly.

She had to twist the pin a bit, rattling it around a bit forcefully, but after a few seconds, she heard the very dry, audible *click* as the lock disengaged. She paused for a moment, a smile on her face, unable to believe that it had worked. She'd expected to have to fight with it for several minutes (if it worked at all) but it had taken her about twenty seconds.

Experimentally, she turned the doorknob. Ava smiled even wider when the door opened easily, allowing her to step into Ronald Amberley's apartment. She waited a moment, though, understanding that she was about to cross a line. Breaking and entering without a warrant was essentially a crime. But then again, she knew the deck was stacked against her. If she was going to close this case on her own, she was going to have skirt some of the rules.

Sighing, Ava stepped inside.

And now that you're in, Clarence's voice spoke up in her head, *you need to move fast. Cop or not, this is still technically breaking and entering. You just said so yourself.*

She stood just inside the doorway for a moment, listening closely and getting a feel for the place. It was clear right away that no one was home. The apartment consisted of a joint kitchen and living room area, a small bathroom, and a bedroom. It was all crammed into a small space and would not provide any room for someone to hide.

The place was also something of a wreck. There were newspapers and pads scattered everywhere, little nubs of pencils littering the kitchen counters and the small table in the den. There were also dirty dishes sitting all about, on the two chairs in the den, and several on what she thought might be a small end table; it was too hard to know for sure because it was buried in newspaper pages.

There were two old chairs that looked like the sort people often placed out in the yard during summer. A small table sat between them, covered in papers and pads. Ava made her way into the bedroom and found that it was much smaller than she'd been expecting. There was barely room for the bed and the small dresser to fit comfortably within it.

The bed was unmade and there were a few scattered clothes on the mattress and in the floor. The top of the dresser was littered with numerous things: a comb, an empty glass, a driver's cap, and a notebook with a few torn pages sticking out. Ava grabbed the notebook and started thumbing through it.

She realized she'd found something of great importance almost right away. Written on the inside of the back cover was Millie's name and the address of the *Brooklyn Eagle*'s newspaper offices. As she thumbed through the pages, she wondered why Ronald Amberley would have Millie's notebook. She supposed it made *some* degree of sense if he had indeed been trailing her, but why not hand it back in to the newspaper? It seemed to highlight the fact that Skinner had not even mentioned Amberley working alongside Millie Newsom and made Ava wonder if there was something deeper going on there.

Looking through the notes, Ava quickly found that Millie was apparently not a laborious note taker. There were numerous note and scribblings, just the sketches and outlines of basic ideas. Here and there, she came across a name or an address, but the majority of them were either marked out or scribbled through.

About three quarters of the way through the notebook, the notes came to an end. Ava studied the final notes Millie Newsom had written down. It was very brief and left a ton of unanswered questions, but there was more than enough to go on. In fact, it was enough to give

Ava chills and a certain feeling of anxiety in her stomach. The final words placed in the notebook were: **Bootlegging at Loose Goose! Mob connection, but who? Guy #1 dead-end. Let's trail Guy #2....seems to be sort of stupid.**

It blew Ava's mind that a journalist who was said to be a brilliant up-and-comer could get anywhere when keeping notes like these. She'd assumed an on-the-rise journalist would have kept pages upon pages of notes, neatly compiled and easy to read. Apparently, she was wrong. That, or Millie Newsom was a very unique creature.

She read the lines a few more times, committing them to memory. As she did, she now realized that she had three potential leads: Ronald Amberley, George Spotnitz of 551 Holloway Street, and now a potential mob or bootlegging connection that could somehow be linked to a place called the Loose Goose. She figured it was a place in Brooklyn that Millie had known. Ava personally had never heard of it...not that it meant much of anything. If there was no jazz there, she'd have no interest in the place anyway.

Ava placed the notebook back on the dresser where she'd gotten it from, again making a note of ask Amberley—if she ever came across him—how he'd ended up with Millie's notebook. Then, after some thought, she decided to take it. If she ever spoke with Amberley, she could use it as evidence. And if it came up later down the road when speaking with Skinner or Minard...well, she'd cross that bridge when she got there.

On her way out, she made sure to lock the door as she left. She considered waiting around for Ronald Amberley but decided against it. She had two other leads to chase down and she wasn't going to waste her time sitting idly by. Back out on the street, she debated who to go after first: the Loose Goose or George Spotnitz. She figured Spotnitz might be difficult to locate, as Millie had clearly wanted the name to be remembered but, at the same time, hidden. And though she had an address, Ava also knew just how rife with information clubs could be. She had an address for Spotnitz and could visit it anytime. But she felt that the story Millie had been working on was closely linked to her death, so that would be the best place to start.

With that in mind, she started walking down unfamiliar streets, hoping to find a friendly face that would be able to direct her to the Loose Goose.

CHAPTER EIGHT

Six minutes before someone knocked on his door, Ronald Amberley was flipping through Millie's notebook. He'd looked through it countless times in the past twenty-four hours, hoping to find an answer to why someone might want Millie dead. He knew Millie was a stubborn broad and had pissed off a lot of the wrong sorts of people, but someone wanting her dead seemed like a bit of a stretch that he could not fathom.

He knew he was heartbroken but was not yet allowing himself to accept it. It wasn't until after her death that Ronald had allowed himself to admit he'd been falling for Millie Newsom. It had started as a huge amount of respect for her because she was so damned good at her job. Then, after seeing how she'd never backed down from any man who told her a woman's place was most certainly not in the newsroom, it had become awe. Shortly after that, after seeing her face and nearly perfect body in action every day, it had become lust. He'd thought that had been the end of it but the emptiness that had been left behind when he'd watched her die in the street had told him it was something else entirely.

He supposed that's why he'd taken the notebook. When he'd first snagged it up and run away, he told himself it was because he wanted to take the case over and finish it for her. But now he wondered if his heart had him take it because he wanted something that had belonged to her.

Whatever the reason had been, he looked through it now, as he'd done countless times since her death. While he could not make heads nor tails of any of her notes, looking at her handwriting made his heart ache. He looked back through old notes, unable to read a few words here and there but also able to connect the things he could read with stories she'd blown wide open.

There were notes from a busted bootlegging operation from a few months back, notes about the two children who had been found dead in the Hudson River, notes about the hatchet killer case from just a few weeks ago…so many notes for stories that had all, in a way, told *her* story.

He sat on his bed and read through it all, finally coming to terms that there would be no real answers here. All he had to go on were the final notes he'd scribbled down, and he'd committed those to memory a few days ago when he'd been assigned to tail her on yet another story. He figured if he wanted to find out why she'd been killed, he may have to follow up with completing the story himself. The only problem with that was that Millie had remained secretive about the finer details of this story all the way up until her death. He did know that Millie had recently been looking into details about how certain dirty Brooklyn cops were getting kickbacks from the mafia to look the other way, but he had no solid evidence that was the lead Millie had been chasing when she'd died.

So really, he had no idea where to start. He supposed he could—

A knock at his front door broke him out of his thoughts. He jumped a bit, nervous and on edge because he'd been expecting the police to come by ever since he'd breezed off from the street where Millie had been shot. There was no question that he would not answer the door. He knew it would seem shady later on—just as shady as the fact that he'd not showed up for work today—but he was still unable to see past the fact that Millie was gone. He'd let the repercussions of his actions fall where they may later. For now, he had to just wrap his head around it.

He paused, waiting for another knock, but it never came. He turned his attention back to the notebook, feeling that he may be losing his mind a bit. He'd been obsessively looking over the contents even though he'd known by last night that there was nothing there. He forced himself to close it, placing it on top of his dresser. He wasn't sure where to start. Probably the Loose Goose, as it was specifically called out in Millie's notes. What he was hung up on at the moment were the identities of the people Millie had referred to as "guy 1" and "guy 2." If he could figure that out, he might be able to figure out a proper starting place.

Thinking this, he heard a slight commotion coming from the living room. He barely heard it at all, but it had him walking to his bedroom doorway, looking into his small living room. He'd nearly stepped out when he heard the noise again, soft and light. It was coming from the left side of the living room. It sounded like someone attempting to push against the wall from the outside, but that made no sense.

It's the window, he thought. *Whoever knocked on the door is trying to get in through the window…*

As far as Ronald knew, the police would not try coming in through the window. Perhaps it was someone else, maybe even the man who had shot Millie. Maybe they knew he'd been trailing behind her and were now coming for him to make sure he couldn't say anything—not that he had anything he *could* say. Still, this was not good. If someone was trying to come in through his window, there was no telling what lengths they might go to.

He hunkered down and crawled out of his bedroom. When he looked to the window, he saw someone walking away from it. He'd just missed them. Apparently, whoever it had been wasn't willing to break a window to get to him. That, at least, was some relief.

He stood motionless for a moment, wanting to head out to the Loose Goose to start his own investigation, but assuming it would be smartest to wait a few minutes—to allow whoever had been at his door and window to get a good distance away. He headed back to get the notebook when he heard footsteps outside his front door. Were they back? Were they maybe going to break the door down this time?

He had a very small apartment, giving him nowhere to hide. But when he heard something rattling around in the lock outside his door, Ronald got desperate and creative. He rushed to the kitchen and opened up one of the three cabinets that ran along under the counter. One of them contained a few canned goods and a sack of flour, but the rest of the space was practically empty. He opened the cabinet door furthest to the left as he heard the rattling in the lock. They were picking his lock, from the sound of it. They could be in at any moment…

At first, he was afraid he was not going to fit into the small space, that the frame of the cabinet door would be too small to accept him. He had to bend his left arm at a painful angle and he whacked his head in the underside of the counter when he finally squeezed himself in, but he *did* fit—just barely. Hunched over so that his knees were nearly touching his chin, he reached back out to close the cabinet door at the very same moment he heard his lock disengaging. He slowly shut the cabinet, making sure it made no noise, as he heard his apartment door swinging open.

From behind the cabinet door, he listened closely. He could hear only one set of footsteps as someone slowly entered his apartment. He was nearly terrified to breathe as they made their way through the kitchen. Surely, they'd open the cabinets at any moment and pull him out.

But the footsteps carried on beyond the kitchen. They were heading into the living room. Unable to help himself, Ronald pushed the cabinet door just the slightest bit with the toe of his shoe. Through the small crack, he could not see much. He saw no face, but he did the see the bottom hem of a long skirt, and a woman's trim legs capped in a pair of simple shoes. This confused him more than anything else and even though the fact that the intruder was a woman relieved him a bit, there was still far too much mystery to just make his hiding spot known. So, as the woman made her way into his bedroom, Ronald slowly drew his foot back, closing the cabinet again.

He sat there uncomfortably, breathing in the dust of the space beneath his counter. He had no idea how much time passed between the moment the woman had entered his apartment and when he heard her footsteps coming back out of his bedroom, but it felt like forever. There was no hesitancy as the woman walked through the kitchen. She was apparently in a hurry to get somewhere else. The question still remained, though: why was she here at all?

Even when he heard the door close, he waited a moment before getting out. He pushed the door open and found it even harder to get out of the small, cramped space. He scraped his arms as he squeezed himself back out onto the kitchen floor and even got his leg tangled in the small door frame at one point.

As he lay there, panting for breath after the effort of getting out of the tiny opening, a thought occurred to him. If the woman had come to his door, then tried the window, and then picked the lock, maybe she was a cop or detective. Maybe she was one of the dirty cops Millie had been writing about. He'd heard a few stories about women cops scattered through the newsroom, most notably out of Manhattan. It made him doubt that a woman cop would be dirty. Besides, a female dick wouldn't be a very good target for mobsters to pay off. Would they?

It was certainly very interesting to say the least. He suddenly wished he *had* come out of his hiding spot while she was there. If she was affiliated with the police, maybe she had answers.

Without much thought, Ronald hurried into his bedroom. He reached for the notebook on top of his dresser, only to find it wasn't there. The woman had taken it. And while this was mildly infuriating, it also made him think the woman may not have been there to silence him at all. No, maybe she was also trying to figure out why someone had seen fit to kill Millie. It was a long shot, but it was one he was willing to take.

Hoping the woman hadn't gotten too far ahead of him, Ronald hurried out of his apartment. He had no idea if he could trust this woman; she had, after all, picked his lock and stolen Millie's notebook. But he was willing to find out, and there was only one way to do that. He was going to hope she hadn't made it too far away from his apartment, and then he would follow her.

CHAPTER NINE

The Loose Goose was located just off the corner of an unremarkable intersection in a part of Brooklyn that was rather quiet as the day crept toward one in the afternoon. She'd had to ask three different people where it was before she had any luck, making her assume it wasn't a very popular place.

When she finally found it, she stopped herself from just barging inside. She knew she could use her background as a jazz singer to have any sort of conversation with the owners; she had some degree of knowledge on how these places were run—even if it was the sort of place that was running a speakeasy out of some hidden rooms. Still, given her recent career path, she knew she had to be careful.

She wasn't too worried about looking out of place. Ever since she'd been promoted to detective, she'd been able to be what the fellows at the precinct referred to as "plainclothes." This allowed her to dress as she would on any given day when she went about businesslike errands and visiting friends and family. It was her gun and badge that she was more concerned with. She figured it may be more to her advantage to go in as a customer rather than a cop. It was going to be far easier to get answers and any clues as to why Millie Newsom had jotted the name of the place down if she went in like an everyday dame.

This would be difficult, though, with a badge and a gun. This was especially true if there *was* a speakeasy on the premises. She knew some places went so far as to pat you down before allowing you into the hidden corners of the places of business. Given this, Ava walked by the Loose Goose when she came to it. She walked a bit farther down the block and stopped when she came to a thin, open alley between a department store and a pharmacist's shop. She stepped into the alley and headed straight for the small garbage bin a little over halfway down the alley. Checking over her shoulder to make sure no one was looking in at her, she stashed her department-issued Smith and Wesson and badge under the bin. After a bit more thought, she also placed Millie Newsom's notebook there as well.

It felt like a foolish thing to do, but she thought she'd be okay. The garbage bin didn't look very full and the chances of anyone coming out and specifically looking under it were slim. Before she could change her mind, Ava exited the alley and headed back to the Loose Goose. When she pushed through the front doors, she did her best to seem as calm as possible.

Inside, the place was a bit nicer than Ava had expected. She supposed it was also because of the early hour on a weekday that there wasn't much activity inside. Just from the look of the place—the décor and the amount of space—Ava assumed it to be a club, but not one that took itself too seriously. There was a stage near the back but it was small and looked as if it had rarely been used. A small counter ran in a U shape along the back corner between the rear and right walls. There were two doors behind the counter and as she walked toward them, she could smell food cooking.

To her left, there were about twenty table settings, some with two chairs and some with as many as five. They were all situated as to leave a circular space open in the center that she supposed served as a dance floor. There were only three other people in the place. Two were sitting together at the counter along the back, eating lunch. The third was sitting at a table by himself, drinking a pop and writing something down in a notebook. He looked at her and then instantly back down at his notebook. He was very shifty-looking, the sort Ava might cross the street to avoid walking by. While she hated to stereotype, she had no problems assuming this man might be affiliated with the mob.

As she came to the counter, she realized that all of the speakeasy terminology was coming back to her. Clarence had mused over some of it whenever he would tell her stories about bootlegging busts, but she knew some from her time at jazz clubs. She'd even indulged here and there, having never been a supporter of prohibition. She brought all of that information to mind as she took a seat at the counter. Of course, this place could be on the up-and-up, but the fact that it was jotted down in Millie's notebook made her doubtful.

A tall, dapper man came out to greet her as soon as she sat down. He smiled widely at her as he wiped his hands on a cloth that hung from his apron.

"Looking for some lunch?" he said.

"A ham sandwich, if you got it."

"Is that all?"

She leaned forward and grinned at him, as if the two were sharing a secret. "Are the tarantulas running loose back there?"

He grinned back and said, "For a price, I think we can make them run." He then eyed her suspiciously, though the grin was still on his face. "Could you pay for something like that?"

"Yes."

"One moment," he said softly. Then, a bit louder: "I'll have that sandwich right out for you, ma'am."

The simple exchange proved that Millie might have been on to something. While Ava did know that a place running a speakeasy didn't automatically link them with the mob, she did know the number of such places was growing by the month. One way or the other, the Loose Goose had been worth looking into.

Ava knew how it all worked and what to expect next. The butter-and-egg man would come out, the man who likely owned the place and signed the checks. He'd invite her somewhere away from other patrons and maybe ask her a few questions. Based on her answers, she'd either be allowed into another room where she'd be served a drink, or she'd be turned away. She found that she wasn't nervous at all; if anything, she was realizing how nice a stiff drink would be. It had been a while since she'd enjoyed one, that was for sure.

Five minutes passed, and the tall waiter came back out with her sandwich and a glass of water. He set it down in front of her and again, they shared the same knowing smile. "Should you need the restroom, it's right around the corner there." He nodded to the right end of the counter where a hallway fed off into another section of the building.

With that said, he took his leave. Ava started on her sandwich and found it quite good, though nothing special. Then again, if the Loose Goose was running a speakeasy, the quality of the food didn't matter all that much, as it wasn't how they were getting most of their money. After a few more bites and a sip or two of water, she got up and headed for the hallway. When she started walking down it, she saw that the restrooms were indeed located along this hall. But before she could reach them, a door all the way at the back of the hallway opened up and an older gentleman stepped out. He was mostly bald and wearing a white-collared shirt with tattered pants. With a grin and a nod, he gestured her toward him and escorted her through the doorway he'd just come out of.

The room Ava stepped into was empty except for a single chair sitting against the wall. Another door sat against this room's right-side wall. It had a padlock along the frame but it was currently unlocked.

"You asked about the tarantulas?" he asked.

"Yes. I asked if they were running. Maybe they've been working on some juice?"

The old man nodded solemnly. "How'd you hear about us?"

"I'm in Brooklyn to see a friend. He stood me up. I asked some guy sitting on his stoop where a good place to eat might be. He asked if I was looking for something wet or dry."

"And you said?"

"Wet."

"You know this man's name?"

"No. Sorry."

He eyed her a bit more before he finally said, "Raise your hands up over your head, would you?"

She did. And though she knew what was coming next, she couldn't help but feel a little violated. The man did his best to remain a gentleman as he frisked her. Ava knew that she was gifted in the chest area, and with her arms above her head pulling tightly against her shirt it was plain to see. The man did his best not to get sidetracked when he reached there, though his eyes did linger a bit. He did not unnecessarily grab her anywhere and he was not rough. And when he was done, he looked rather embarrassed about the ordeal.

"And you have money?"

She nodded and patted her pocket. "Not much, but enough for a few."

"Good enough then," the old man said. He pulled open the door behind him and revealed a larger, darker room. "Walk past the deli meats and hang a left. And watch your step."

She entered the room and noticed that it was lit only by a single overhead bulb. From first glance, it appeared to be a storage room. It was quite cold, and there were racks along the back wall with bottles of pop, some assorted vegetables, and a few packages of uncut deli meat. Following the old man's orders, Ava walked behind the rack of deli meat. When she did, she thought he'd played a trick on her, as there appeared to be nowhere else to go. But in the back, hidden in the darkness and shadows, there was another door. It was very thin, no larger than a closet door, and a very thin sliver of light escaped from the bottom crease.

Ava walked toward it, realizing that the old man was behind her. There was the slightest moment when she was afraid he might attack her but at the last moment, he stepped ahead of her and opened the small door for her. As Ava started to take in the small yet cozy room, the old man spoke up from behind her.

"This one's good," he said before turning on his heel and heading back to the storage room.

There were two men sitting at a scarred table, both drinking from dark bottles. They were well-dressed and one of them wore a fedora low down on his head. They both wore nice suit coats and she could see without even looking hard that there was a bulge beneath one—a concealed gun without a doubt. She thought they may be in cahoots with the man back in the club area who had been sucking a pop and jotting down something in his notebook.

Beyond these two potential mobsters, there was what looked like a very large desk tucked all the way back along the wall. A man stood there, nervously watching her enter. Wanting to look as if she belonged there and that she wasn't nervus herself, she walked up to him.

"Moonshine, whiskey, or beer?" he asked.

"Beer."

He reached behind the odd mixture of table and desk. She could hear ice being shifted around and he then placed a dark bottle, the top already popped, on the table. "That'll be a buck."

She'd expected a steep price, but this wasn't as bad as what she'd heard from some other speakeasies. Clarence had told her stories of people charging up to five dollars for a quart of rotgut homemade liquor. She took the money from her pocket, doing her best to pretend it wasn't a bit painful to spend it.

She sipped from it and found the taste appalling—almost like copper at first. But then once it was down it was quite nice, just bitter.

"Thanks," she said, tipping the bottle at him.

"O' course. Nice to see a lady down here and every so often. Your fella know you're here?"

"I don't have a fella." Then, to add to her authenticity, she added: "He died not too long ago."

"Sorry to hear it."

"I think he would have supported me coming here, though. There don't seem to be many in Brooklyn, huh?"

"Oh, there are a few. And prices keep going up."

"You'd think it would keep people from showing up. You get a lot of traffic here?" She continued drinking the beer. She couldn't believe she'd been so appalled by the first sip. It was going down a bit too easily as she spoke to the man.

"Some," he said. "Not too much."

She wasn't sure if it was just her imagination or not, but Ava was pretty sure she saw the would-be bartender giving a quick glance to the two men who were sitting behind her. She turned in their direction, bottle still raised to her lips, and saw that the two men at the table were standing.

"You see, doll," the bartender said, "some of that traffic we get, it tells us about coppers, and what to watch out for. And they mentioned a lady cop, some hotshot skirt that might be sniffing around. Said she's making headlines, making a name for herself."

Her eyes were still on the mobsters (she was now certain that's what they were) as the bartender said all of this. The one who was clearly packing was a beast of a man, though most of his heft seemed to be an abundance of weight, not muscle. The other stood as still as a stone, staring her down. Facing Ava, he said: "That wouldn't happen to be you, would it?"

Ava eyed the door behind them. It was close enough where she could make a run for it if she had to. But then she saw a third man—a man she had not seen when she'd first been escorted into this room. She couldn't help but wonder if even the man up front who had served her sandwich had known why she was there. Maybe she'd been led back here like a lamb to the slaughter.

This third man was built like a brick shithouse (an old saying Clarence had liked to use). He stood in front of the door with his arms folded, as if daring her to come at him.

"I don't want any trouble," she said. This was very far from the truth. She had never minded making trouble. She was just trying to make them feel confident while buying some time.

"That's a shame," the overweight mobster said. "Because we're going to give you some."

He went for his gun and when Ava made her first move, it was by nothing more than instinct. The world became a single swirling image as Ava was forced to fight for her life, well aware that the passing of the next few seconds could mean she'd not close this case and end up just as dead as Millie Newsom.

CHAPTER TEN

Frank Wimbly had always preferred to work alone...but then Ava Gold had come along.

He wished he hadn't come forward with his feelings about her so quickly. Now that he'd done it, he could look back and see that the timing was all off. And now that they had been separated for a few days, he worried that it might put a strain on their working relationship.

Currently, Frank was sitting in a waiting area outside of a pretentious Wall Street office. Even the little waiting area seemed far too classy. It was so classy it looked fake—which, as far as Frank was concerned, was mostly true of all the Wall Street cake eaters he'd ever come into contact with. Some big shot had been killed last night and there were three brokers arguing over who might have done it. The poor sap had been shot right in the back of the head outside of his apartment. His lovely young wife had found him missing most of his head and she had a few opinions on who the killer might be, too. The fact that everyone he was speaking to in regards to the case was filthy rich and entitled beyond measure made things so much worse.

He was thinking of Ava and wondering how she might be handling herself in Brooklyn when the man he'd been waiting to see finally came out of his office. His name was Earl Spencer and the suit he was wearing likely cost more than every single article of clothing Frank owned.

"Sorry to keep you waiting," Spencer said. "But this murder on top of all of these stock prices in chaos is making things crazy around here."

"It's fine," Frank said. "And I'll try not to take up too much of your time."

He followed Spencer into his large office. Frank hated how envious he was of it. Never one for riches or the finer things, Frank had always been a man of simplicity. But damn, it would be nice to have the luxuries of Earl Spencer. The man settled in behind his desk as if he were about to drive a boat. It was a massive slab of an oak desk and it seemed to fit him well.

"I have three names," Frank said. "And to be quite blunt with you, I just need to know your gut reaction as to whether or not they might have had it in them to kill your old employee, Victor D'Amour."

"If they work for me, I can tell you right now the answer is no."

"They don't currently work for you, but two have within the past year and a half."

"Forgive me for saying so, Detective, but this feels a bit like a witch hunt."

Frank laughed ironically and shook his head. "You're forgiven. And it's not a witch hunt. It's a police investigation. Given the number of people in the financial sector that have been dying—some by their own hands, I've noticed—I'd think you'd want this sort of thing solved quickly."

"What are the names?" Spencer asked, clearly irritated.

Frank gave him the names, reciting them off as if they were of no real consequence or importance. He hated that he was so distracted by Ava's current situation. More than that, he hated that he was finding it harder and harder to garner sympathy for a murder victim who lived and breathed the Wall Street lifestyle. Put those two things together and this whole case suddenly seemed like a recipe for disaster.

Spencer considered the names, though he didn't look particularly worried. Frank supposed he understood. Over the past six to eight months, it seemed there had been a lot of deaths concerning the Wall Street crowd. It was almost becoming just another expected part of the job.

"I'm not telling you how to do your job, Detective," Spencer said with far too much smugness in his voice, "but you're going to waste your time looking into those three men. I can personally vouch for two of them and the other is so worried about his image and stature that murder would be the *last* thing I'd expect him to be guilty of."

"Well, do you have any names? And, for that matter, were you surprised to hear that Victor D'Amour had been murdered?"

"It may sound cruel, but no…not really. Victor had a penchant for rubbing people the wrong way."

"Did he ever rub *you* the wrong way, Mr. Spencer?"

The question came automatically. He was too worried about Ava and her case. He was also a little irritated that Captain Minard had signed off on it. Ava might be very intelligent and quick-witted, but this was a dangerous situation. He could understand the messed up

51

mentality of trying to set her up to fail, but this case she had out in Brooklyn could even prove to be deadly.

Somehow, he made it through the line of questioning with Spencer in a mostly professional manner. Honestly, it had really only been a ruse. He was going to check up on the three names he'd given Spencer; he only wanted to see if Spencer would be forthcoming with any incriminating evidence against the three men before Frank found it himself.

As he made his way out of the building, Frank found himself wondering if there might be anyone he knew at the precinct who had connection with the unit down in Brooklyn. Would there be any way for him to get an update on Ava's progress, or just to make sure she was safe? For that matter, would anyone ever find out if he decided to head over there himself to make sure she was okay? Or that she wasn't being bullied or harassed the same way some of the men in his own precinct had done when she'd first started.

He didn't think it was worth the risk. He was confident that Ava could handle herself. And besides that, there was no way to inquire about such a thing without seeming overly concerned. With the way things were at the precinct now, that was the last thing he needed. Not only did he not want anyone else knowing his true feelings for her, but she'd likely be given an even harder time if it became public knowledge. It would, of course, not be her fault but he knew how the male brain worked.

With no way to check in on Ava, he did the next best thing he could do. He started heading to the address of the first man on his list so his brain could try to focus on something else.

CHAPTER ELEVEN

She wasn't too bothered by the fact that she didn't have a gun. If she shot all three of these men, and maybe even the bartender, that was going to create more problems than it was going to solve. Besides, she still felt much more comfortable with her fists; she'd not yet learned to trust the weight and power of a gun.

When the fat mobster went for the gun concealed beneath his coat, Ava's instincts took over. Her first move seemed silly and ridiculous as she moved to do it but paid off right away. She reached out with both hands and grabbed the side of the table the men had been sitting behind. With one fluid motion, she flipped it over. Bottles went to the floor, shattering and spilling out their illegal contents. As she'd expected, the motion took them both off guard. The overweight man stumbled back, seemingly forgetting that he'd been going for his gun. His hand paused as he nearly stumbled to his rear end.

While he was mixed up, Ava took a single stride forward and delivered one of the most vicious right hooks she'd ever dished out directly to the side of the second man's head. She could feel in her posture and delivery that she was executing a perfect boxer's stance. She could also tell by the way he dropped that he was out cold and whatever happened here next, he would no longer be part of the problem.

"Hey!" the bartender shouted. It was a comical declaration, the sound of a boy who had just picked a fight and realized he may not win.

Ava turned toward him just long enough to ensure he did not have a gun. When she saw he did not, she turned her attention to the doorman and the overweight mobster. The mobster had finally remembered what he'd been in the middle of doing when the table had been flipped over and he was going for his gun again. Ava knew a gut punch would do very little and, with one hand occupied with the gun, he'd not be able to properly block a head punch. So that's exactly what she delivered. He managed to sidestep just a bit, throwing her aim off. Rather than clocking him in the temple, she connected with the spot just between his earlobe and jaw.

The man yelped and once again seemed conflicted with what to do, clasp the side of his head in pain or go for the gun. As he tried to make this decision, the doorman came charging at her. She saw that he was also not armed, but a man of his size could do potentially more damage with just his fists.

Surprising him *and* the fat mobster, Ava kneed the mobster in the crotch. When he bent over as she'd expected, she grabbed him around the neck and, in a move that felt childlike in the moment, pivoted around him as if she'd been hiding behind a tree. It confused the doorman just enough for her to get a moment's beat on him. She delivered a punch that landed squarely along his solar plexus. It was like hitting a slab of marble. Her wrist bent back painfully but she saw that the blow had at least knocked him back a bit. And that was all she needed.

She wasn't here for a fight. She'd come to find out any information she could about the place. Besides, one of the strengths of any good boxer was to know when you might be outmatched by another fighter. And while Ava thought she might be able to hold her own against the doorman, she wasn't particularly interested in finding out.

Taking advantage of the doorman's momentary shock, Ava dashed for the door. She glanced back in time to see the bartender coming around his little makeshift bar with a wooden baseball bat. He was carrying it as if he'd never held it with the intention of hurting anyone, but that, to Ava, didn't make him any less dangerous.

She reached to open the door and at the very last minute, felt something like a harsh burning along the back of her scalp. When her head was yanked backwards, she realized someone had grabbed her hair and was pulling hard. She cried out and fell into it, hoping to stagger whoever was pulling her hair.

She wasn't too surprised to see that it was the doorman. He had her hair in one hand and as he spun her toward him, his other hand—his left, which was balled into a tremendous fist—was drawing back for a punch. Knowing that she would not get her full strength into a punch, Ava delivered a kick to the side of his right leg. Her aim was true, and the man staggered and then fell to the floor. She had not time to feel relief at this, though, as the bartender was there, bat drawn back as if he were trying out for the Yankees.

Fortunately, he was slow and unsteady with the bat. She waited for him to swing and ducked it easily. When she came up, she delivered two punches—one to the kidneys and one straight into the stomach.

The bartender drew in a gasp and dropped the bat as he fell to the floor. Ava scooped the bat up easily, and just in time, too; the doorman was already getting to his feet, favoring the right knee she'd kicked.

Not interested in killing anyone, Ava drew the bat back and swung at his stomach. When he blocked it, she used it to jab him in the ribs. A sickening *crack* told her that she'd broken at least one rib. The man went to the floor hard, gasping and moaning. Ava surveyed the room once more and saw that the only remaining threat was the overweight mobster. He was trying to get to his feet, cupping his balls and swaying against the wall. When Ava approached him, he cringed and started to move his hands to defend himself. Another well-aimed right hook dropped him just as easily as his mob buddy.

Her right hand was throbbing and she was starting to think she may have very well damaged her wrist on that first blow to the doorman. Still, she turned to the bartender, not certain how long the doorman would stay down.

"What do you know about a journalist that may have come through here?" Ava asked. "It was a woman named Millie Newsom."

"What journalist?" he asked. He was absolutely terrified, surely not having expected the ass-beating she'd just doled out. She wasn't sure she'd ever seen a man so scared of her and she wasn't sure if she felt comfortable with how much she enjoyed it.

"I just told you. Millie Newsom. She was killed yesterday and her notes mentioned the Loose Goose."

"I have no idea what you mean," he whined. "I swear. You're the first woman I've seen back here in at least a few months!"

"And just how often are you here?"

"Almost every day! I swear...I don't know anything about a journalist."

She checked the other three men. The doorman was the only one showing any signs of getting to his feet. She guessed she had another fifteen or twenty seconds.

"You aren't lying to me, are you?"

"No! I swear! It must be the rival outfit."

"What do you mean by *rival outfit*?"

"I thought you would know. I thought you—"

He was interrupted by the sound of the hidden door opening. Ava was ready to fight further if she had to, even if it was the old man who had led her back here. But she saw someone new at the doorway, a man she'd not seen yet. When he saw the shape of the room, his eyes widened and he took off.

Again working on pure instinct, Ava turned her attention to the fleeing man. The bartender seemed truly clueless, and she knew she'd get no information from the mobsters. This new man was running, which suggested guilt. And from the look of fear she'd seen on his face, she didn't think she'd have much trouble catching him.

With a final look back at the carnage she'd caused, Ava ran for the door. The doorman made one final, failed attempt to reach out and stop her, but it was half-hearted at best. Ava barely even saw him. Her attention was now turned back toward that dark storage room and the sounds of the man ahead of her, trying to escape.

CHAPTER TWELVE

Ava was running with such speed and was being pushed by such a surge of adrenaline that she nearly collided with the rack of deli meats when she was back in the darkened storage room. She managed to skid around it while keeping her eyes ahead of her. At the door of the storage room that led back out into the main hallway of the Loose Goose, she saw the man who had taken off running as he haphazardly pushed the old, balding man to the side.

He was stumbling against the wall as Ava passed by him, her eyes still on the running man ahead of her, and her legs reminding her that she was still being chased. She came out into the hallway just as the man was rounding the corner into the larger room, sprinting to the left in the direction of the door.

Ava did her best to recall the people who had been sitting in this room when she arrived, wondering if any of them would give her ay problems. She thought of the man with his soda and notebook, still wondering if he, too, was connected to the mob. She kept her eyes peeled for him as she came into the room but she saw that he was gone; the only thing remaining was his empty soda bottle.

Ahead of her, the front door opened. The daylight that spilled through gave her the first real glimpse of the man she was chasing. He looked to be on the younger side. Dressed in a frumpy white T-shirt and a pair of worker's pants, he looked as if he'd thrown on the same clothes he'd worn the day before. His hair standing up in disarray did not help his appearance either. He took off to the right and Ava chased after him. He was fast, but his fear was causing him to move a bit frantically, which made his steps shaky and uneven. By the time Ava had passed through the front door and reached the street, she'd cut the distance between them nearly in half.

She was so focused on chasing this young man down that the pain in her wrist seemed to subside. She was even able to momentarily push the events of her fight in the speakeasy back room aside as she continued to close the gap between them. When she drew to within ten feet of him, she found it both ironic and funny that he quickly slid into the alleyway between the department store and pharmacist's shop—the very same alley she'd ventured down to hide her gun and badge.

She rounded the same corner and saw that he had slowed a bit to catch his breath. When he saw Ava come barreling around the side of the building, his eyes grew wide again, and he picked up the pace again. But by then, it was too late. Before he could get going good, Ava was able to reach out and grab his arm. When she spun him around against the wall of the department store, he cried out and threw his hands in the air.

"Okay, okay, I'm sorry!" he said.

Ava pinned him against the wall and her wrist reminded her that it had been tweaked. She managed to fight past it, though, not wanting to show this man any weakness. Not that it mattered. He was fairly young—surely no older than twenty-five—and had a thin, frail frame. He looked tired and terrified, perhaps afraid that Ava would deal with him the same way she'd dealt with the men in the speakeasy.

Putting all of this together in her head, Ava suddenly knew who she was looking at. The man she had pinned to the wall was the man who had been trailing behind Millie Newsom. It was the man who lived in the apartment she'd broken into less than half an hour ago.

"Are you Ronald Amberley?" she asked.

"Yeah…" he said, clearly confused as to how she could know this.

"What the hell were you doing in there?"

"Looking for a drink."

His voice was thin and doubtful, essentially painting the lie for him. Even if his voice had not betrayed him, Ava simply did not think he looked like the type to hit up a speakeasy so early in the afternoon—if at all.

"I don't buy that for a second," she said. "Why are you following me?"

"Because I wanted to know why you broke into my apartment." He apparently read her look of confusion, because he then said: "I was there, hiding. I waited a bit before coming out and followed you after you left."

She relaxed her grip on him but remained in an offensive position just in case he decided to try running again.

"Were you with Millie Newsom when she was killed?" Ava asked.

It was clear that he *wanted* to answer, but was struggling to say anything; she could see it in the tension on his face and the loosening of his lips. "You took the notebook from my place," he said.

"I did. I'm a detective, looking into Millie's death. I suppose the better question, though, is why you ran from the scene with her notebook. You were with her when it happened, weren't you? Did you really see nothing?"

"You're a detective?" he asked, a little shocked. "Can you prove it?"

"I can," she said. She walked several yards to the left, to the garbage bin where she'd stashed her holstered sidearm and badge on the ground, under the bin. She placed the holster back along her waist, making sure to hide it with the thin long-sleeved top she wore over her shirt. She then brushed off her badge and showed it to Amberley. "Detective Ava Gold. Any other questions?"

He seemed perplexed by this, still opting to remain silent. Ava used his silence to her advantage, throwing out a few more of her own.

"Why were you following me?"

"Because you broke into my apartment, and I wanted to know why."

"A woman who worked with Millie gave me your name. She believed you had been trailing her for a story. But oddly enough, your chief editor never mentioned it. And your name isn't in the police report anywhere. That's why I broke into your apartment. I needed answers because, quite frankly, this case is starting to feel pretty slippery. I'm sort of against the wall here…and I'm not about to get into the details of it with you right now. If you desperately need the notebook, you can have it."

"Where is it?"

Ava nodded back to the garbage bin. "Under there. I didn't pull it out right away because I wasn't trying to play all of my cards at once. You can have it back, but I really need you to cooperate. I need some answers."

"I'll gladly tell you whatever you want," Amberley said. "I want her killer captured more than anyone. But I don't really trust the cops. No offense. There are some things that have gone down as of late that make me wary of anyone with a gun and a badge."

"Does it help at all that I'm not out of Brooklyn?"

"A bit. Where are you from?"

"Manhattan. I was sent down here to…well, to *help*." She did her best to keep the irritation out of her voice. The last thing she wanted to do was spook her one strong lead in the case.

"So can I trust you?" Amberley asked.

"Yes. As far as I'm concerned, you and I want the same thing. I have to say, though, I'm half-inclined to arrest you."

"Me? You're the one breaking into people's apartments and going into a speakeasy to kick every ass in the place. Why would you arrest me?"

"For not coming forward even when you were right there when she died. For running away. For taking her personal property in the form of that notebook."

"Fine, okay. What do you need to know?"

"Everything," Ava said. "But not here. I'd really rather be as far away from here as possible when those men back in the speakeasy are able to walk again. Grab the notebook and let's get out of here."

Amberley did as she asked, but was hesitant to take his eyes off of her. It was clear that he didn't quite trust her to change her mind and give him a beating as well. Ava took a few steps back, giving him his space. She looked down the alleyway, making sure no one was coming for them. She kept her fists clenched even though her right one was swelling a bit, ready to fight again if she had to.

In the end, no one came. Amberley got the notebook from beneath the garbage bin and they left the alley without any trouble. Together, they left the Loose Goose behind but Ava could still feel its shadow on her as they left, making her think her business there might not be completely done.

CHAPTER THIRTEEN

Ronald Amberley was beyond impressed with Ava Gold. It was more than the fact that she'd somehow bested four men in the back of a speakeasy. He'd only seen the very end of that exchange, after all. And it wasn't only how fast she was, able to catch up to him with no problem after he'd chosen to run. No, it was something else—some hidden confidence that seemed to come out of her every movement. Even as they traversed the streets of Brooklyn, taking a series of random lefts and rights at intersections as they got farther and farther away from the Loose Goose, he could see it. He wasn't sure if he completely trusted her yet, but he did feel safe with her.

They came to a stop at a small, greasy spoon. The place was about half full of patrons and the air was thick with the smell of cooked meat and coffee. They took a seat at a booth that was not by a window and were greeted almost immediately by a waitress. They both ordered coffees and the waitress flitted off quickly to get them.

"Okay, so you have the notebook," Ava said. "All I want is information. I need as much as you can give me. This final story Millie was working on...I'm being told it might have been about bootlegging, or a more specific piece about the mob. Can you clear that up?"

"It was about bootlegging, but also how the mob has really started to play a role in how it's being handled in most parts of the city. And while any journalist is going to be a little nervous writing up a piece that involves the mob, this one went somewhere Millie wasn't expecting. She didn't give me full details, but I do know that she learned about a new outfit that was making its presence known here in Brooklyn. They're edging in on a local mafia family's territory. And when she learned about that, Millie seemed to get a little more secretive than usual. I'm pretty sure there at the end, she resented the fact that I'd been tasked to trail her."

"Had she been able to identify anyone in this new outfit?"

The waitress arrived with their coffee, breaking up the conversation. She asked if they wanted any food and when they both shook their heads, she walked away quickly. Amberley sipped from his coffee, wondering if it was smart to tell Gold everything. It might endanger her, for all he knew. But when he recalled the sight he'd walked into back at the speakeasy, he felt certain she could handle herself.

"She *thought* she had," he finally answered. "We were trailing him yesterday just before she was shot."

"What's his name?"

Again, he seemed to be wrestling with whether or not to tell her. When he finally did get it out, he lowered his head a bit. "Clay Johnson."

"You're sure?"

"Yes. Positive."

"She got this guy's name, located him, and then both of you followed him?"

"Yeah. We were following him for about ten minutes before the shot came."

"So was he the shooter?"

He opened his mouth to respond in the affirmative, but thought better of it. He'd been going through the scene in his head for the past twenty-four hours and no matter how badly he wanted to be able to point Clay Johnson out, the sad fact of the matter remained that he never saw the creep pull the trigger.

"I can't say with certainty that it was him," he said. "I did not see him turn around with a gun and I did not see him pull a trigger. But it seems odd, doesn't it, that the shot came while we were following him?"

"I'd agree," Ava said. "I visited the scene of the shooting. There weren't many places for a shooter to hide. Did you get a good look at Johnson *after* the shot?"

"Yeah, I did. He took off running…like he was trying to get away."

"Or, if he *is* with the mob, maybe the sound of a gunshot simply spooked him and he took off. We can't just *assume* he's the killer."

"And this is why I don't trust cops," Amberley said. "Sure, no one saw him pull the trigger but the entire scenario suggests it, right?"

"Yes. And I'd say it's enough to question him, but not to arrest him. That being said, do you happen to know where I can find him?"

"I do. And I'll be happy to show you."

He watched as she sipped her coffee, thinking about it. But when she put her cup back down on the table, Ava shook her head. "No. I can't have a civilian getting into it that deep. Especially not a civilian who has already made up their mind about the suspect."

"If I don't go, I don't tell."

"That's a shame. You seem like a nice enough man. I'd hate to arrest you for admitted interference in a case."

"You wouldn't!"

Ava shrugged. "Do you want to find her killer or what?"

She was a tough bird, that was for sure. "I do, but…hold on. How about this?" He placed Millie's notebook on the table and tapped it with a thin finger. "Could you make much sense out of this?"

"Lord no. She writes in incomplete sentences and some of the handwriting is atrocious."

"All true. But I can read all of it, even the horrible chicken scratch handwriting."

"And?"

"I can translate it for you. Anything you need to know that's on here and illegible, I can help you figure it out."

"Nice try, but it seems to me the only thing I need to know is on that final page. I was able to read *Loose Goose* and that turned out to be something. I appreciate the gesture, Ronald, I really do. But I just can't have you come along. Now…if you want me to look into this Clay Johnson character, you're going to have to tell me where I can find him."

She'd called his bluff without even really trying. He felt defeated, but at the same time, still like he might be in good hands with Ava Gold. He had no idea what sort of issues she might be having in Manhattan that had sent her here to Brooklyn, but he thought it might have something to do with why she seemed so unstoppable—so *capable.*

He had one more ploy. It was absolutely true, but he'd really hoped to not have to admit to it. "She's all I had," he said. "She had no idea, but I was falling in love with her. It was weird because I also looked up to her and wanted to be as good at the job as she was. I have to be able to help find her killer."

"You can. Tell me where to find Clay Johnson. And if he's not the killer, then maybe he'll provide a path to the next person in the line."

He picked up his coffee, though he really didn't want any more. He sipped it listlessly, accepting that Gold was not going to budge on this.

So sure…he'd tell her.

But he was also going to follow her. She hadn't noticed when he'd tailed her from his apartment, so why would this be any different? He remembered thinking earlier on that he must not be the best at following people in secret but he was starting to understand how very wrong and misguided that had been.

"We've only ever heard it referred to as the Duck Pond. If all of the hushed whispers and rumors are correct, it's an underground distillery. And Clay Johnson is supposedly a big player."

"Great. That's perfect. Where is it?"

"It's somewhere in the Italian Quarter. I can give you the block it's supposed to be hidden on, but I don't have an exact location."

"There's not even one in here?" Ava asked, looking to Millie's notebook.

"No. I don't even know if Millie knew. But…if I tell you where it's supposed to be, how certain are you that you can find out who did this?"

"Nothing's certain with this job," Ava said. "But I can give you my word that I will try my absolute best."

Amberley met her gaze across the table and felt an odd sort of relief. He wasn't sure if it had come from her tone of voice or from the resolute look on her face, but he believed her.

CHAPTER FOURTEEN

Ava found it both odd and fitting that her case in Brooklyn was taking her back toward Manhattan. She was vaguely familiar with the Italian Quarter—better known as Little Italy—because it occupied a slice of lower Manhattan and her brief career with the NYPD had taken her there during routine patrols. Clarence had also spoken highly of the place, as he'd always been taken by Italian culture—namely the cuisine.

As she took a cab into lower Manhattan, she started to understand the danger she was potentially putting herself in. Someone had told the people running the speakeasy out of the Loose Goose about a female detective. She wondered if it was a warning that was now widespread or if it was just being passed around through certain tight circles. It also made her wonder if word had gotten out in Brooklyn because she was on this case. That seemed to make more sense, but it did open up any other questions—namely, who could possibly know? The only people that knew she was on the Millie Newsom case were Captain Skinner, the cops who had originally run with the case, Albert Palmer of the *Brooklyn Eagle* and now Ronald Amberley.

Still, word was getting out somehow, and she wondered if that word may have reached the ears of the men working at what Amberley had referred to as the Duck Pond. If so, she could be walking into a very risky situation. Because of this, her nerves were on high alert when the cab pulled to the curb and she paid her fare. She stepped out into a relatively quiet street. There were some pedestrians, a few of whom were huddled around a small stand where a shoeshine boy was hard at work.

She walked a slow circuit of the block Ronald Amberley had directed her to. It was unremarkable in just about every way. On the stretch she'd been dropped off on, she saw the usual collection of businesses: a small grocer, a tailor, a dry goods store, and a small business called Classy that seemed to cater to only women's makeup and hair accessories. Around the corner, there was more of the same. She passed by a sundry station and a paint store before walking in front of what appeared to be another department store. From the look of the empty display window and the bars over the doors, it was apparently no longer in business.

She hesitated here because it seemed like the ideal sort of place for someone to run an illegal distillery. She continued walking, not wanting to draw any unnecessary attention to herself. She figured she'd walk around to the other side of the block and see if there was a back lot behind the abandoned shop.

As she walked, she realized she'd made up her mind. After passing a very small diner, a barbershop, and a plumber's shop, she was quite sure the abandoned store was the only place on the block worth looking into. It didn't necessarily scream any sort of suspicion, but since Ava knew exactly what she was looking for, it fit the bill.

When she came to the other side of the block, she saw that there was indeed an alleyway that also served as a secondary side street. As she started down it, she saw a light duty pickup parked behind the plumber's store. The back tailgate was down and she saw several lengths of pipe waiting to be unloaded. She looked away, though, looking to her right. She saw the back of the abandoned store, a thin stretch of pavement behind it that connected it to the other businesses. There was a loading door all the way to the right, and several standard doors all along the rear of the building.

She walked briskly across the stretch of pavement, not going out of her way to appear as if she were sneaking around. If anything, she wanted to look as if she had every reason in the world to be there, behind that abandoned business at about five o'clock in the afternoon. She checked each of the doors along the back and found them locked. As she tried each one, she did find it odd that the knobs all looked rather new. It rang some alarms in her head because it made no sense to replace knobs and locks in a building that was, for all intents and purposes, abandoned.

She then went to the loading door. It was well-worn and beaten, an accordion-style door with a handle at the bottom. She reached down to grab it but just as her fingers fell on it, a noise from directly beside her made her freeze.

It was the sound of a gun being cocked.

"Step away, little miss," a brooding male voice said.

Ava felt the weight of the Smith and Wesson holstered at her waist. She knew that going for it would be foolish, though. She had no clear view of the man who had gotten the jump on her so she was at an automatic disadvantage.

Still bent over, Ava took a shuffling step away from the door.

"Good girl," the man said. "Now stand up straight."

As she did as he'd instructed, she finally saw the man. He was standing to her right, having come from beside the corner of the building, where it met alongside the paint store.

"Lace your hands behind your back."

Ava did this, too. "I'm sorry," she said. "I think I might be lost and—"

"Quiet," the man said. He had a brooding face that matched his voice. His nose looked like it had been broken at some point, and his eyes were mostly hidden by the driver's cap he wore low on his brow. As Ava studied him, he kicked at the loading door. "Open it up, Stan!"

Right away, the loading door opened, rolling up in the tracks along the frame. As it rolled up, Ava saw the interior. There was an old storage room beyond it, all of the shelves empty except for dust and grime. A door in the back of the room was opened, leading into a dark room that reminded her of the storage room back at the Loose Goose.

"Good job, Nick," the man inside—Stan presumably—said. "Found us a tasty little dish, did you?"

"Sure did. I sure would like a taste, that's for sure." He gave her a nudge with his gun, a new and shining revolver. "Inside."

"Oh, I think maybe we need to take to her to Clay before we taste anything," Stan said.

"Oh, for sure. He still in?"

"Yeah. And he'll be happy to see such a pretty little thing."

"Look," Ava said, noting that one of them had mentioned someone named Clay. "This is all a mistake. I swear, it's—"

"Might as well shut those pretty lips and save that," Nick said. "Hopefully the boss will be in a good mood today."

"But—"

This time, Nick clocked her right between the shoulder blades with the butt of his revolver. "Shut that mouth of yours before I fill it with the barrel of my gun."

Stan chuckled and said, "I can think of something better to fill it with."

Nick ignored this as he shoved her forward. "Through the door. Go or I *will* shoot you."

Ava didn't think he would. It was apparently very important to them that she made it to their boss before they chose her fate. She walked forward, trying to decide if she should try to get out of this. The one named Nick still had his gun on her but she had no idea if Stan was armed or not. She decide to just be obedient for now, assuming the Clay they were taking her to was the Clay Johnson that Amberley had mentioned to her.

The room they escorted her into was a makeshift office. There was an old desk in the center and a few piles of papers in the floor and on the edge of the desk. There was a man sitting behind the desk, reclining in his chair and drinking from a clear bottle. The liquid inside was also clear, and Ava was quite certain it was not water.

When he saw Ava, he sat up and put the bottle down. He was a surprisingly handsome man, well-groomed black hair making him look almost enterally young, though she guessed him to be in his late forties. He had a chiseled jawline and a defined brow that instantly made her think of a defiant boxer's stare. Dressed in a refined suit, he looked like he was about to hit the town for an entertaining night.

He wasted no time, sitting forward and steepling his fingers on his desk. "We saw you pass by the front, you know," he said. "When you came walking back here, we figured you were looking for something. So tell me right now…who the hell are you and why are you here?"

She had the lie at the ready, reminding herself that in their cockiness, neither Stan nor Nick had frisked her. Maybe they assumed it was a ridiculous thought that a woman would have a gun on her.

"I'm Vivian Clearwater," she said, drumming up the name of a woman her father had dated for a while after they'd lost her mother. "I'm a reporter for the *Times*."

"And what are you doing here?" the man asked. Though he had not introduced himself, Ava assumed this was indeed Clay Johnson.

"I was friends with Millie Newsom. She was shot yesterday and I'm trying to find out why."

"Is that so?" He looked very concerned now. He got to his feet, keeping his fingers steepled together in front of him. "And how did you know to come looking for me?"

"She'd given me your name that very same morning. She said she was looking into you and your possible connection to something called the Duck Pond."

"Did she know what the Duck Pond is?"

"No," Ava said, doing her best to keep playing the part and keeping the lies smooth and without pause. "But she'd made the assumption based on rumors. It's a distillery, right? And your name is Clay Johnson?"

He laughed nervously, eyeing Stan and Nick as they remained standing behind her. "Yes, all of that is true. But the most burning question is how did Millie Newsom know these things?"

"I have no idea. She was very loyal. She never told anyone who her sources were."

Clay considered this for a moment, taking in a deep breath and letting it out in a sigh. "Here's the thing with journalists: I never know whether or not to believe them. Tell me…what else do you know about the Duck Pond and what happened to Ms. Newsom yesterday?"

"All I know is she was trailing you and then she was shot and killed. You have to understand how that looks, right?"

"Of, of course. And truth be told, Mrs. Clearwater, I don't blame you for assuming I killed her. But I assure you, it was not me. I was just as scared as anyone else on that street when the shot was fired. And here's another truth for you. I had no idea who she was until someone told me last night. I had no idea she was a reporter, though I did know she'd been following me for a while yesterday."

Naturally, Ava had no idea if he was telling the truth or not. She rather hoped he *was*, though. If he was telling the truth, that meant that this rival outfit had no idea that Millie had been on to them. And based on his acceptance of her lie, he also had no idea that she could potentially be a detective coming to snoop around as she had feared.

"How many people know you are here?" Clay asked.

"A few. My editor and another journalist."

"Do they knew where you were headed?"

She had to hesitate here a moment, trying to decide which answer may serve her best. If she said no, she might make it out of this alive. They may let her go with the promise of not giving away their location and what they were doing here. If she said yes, though…well, that would make things stickier for both of them.

"No," she finally answered. "I'm pretty sure I'm the only one Millie told about the Duck Pond. I figure she kept it a secret for a reason."

"And you're really a reporter?"

"Yes."

He smiled and said, "Do all reporters wear guns?" He then looked to Nick and Stan with a scowl on his handsome face. "Did neither of you morons bother to frisk her? I know she's a treat on the eyes, but you have to keep your wits about you at all times. Now…take that pea shooter off of her and get her out of here."

Stan worked quickly to remove the gun from her waist. He left the holster and simply took the gun. He seemed flustered, as if he was very embarrassed this was something they'd neglected to do.

"Do we…take her to the place?" Nick asked.

"Yes. Take her away from here and take care of her." When he looked to Ava, she nearly believed him when he said: "I'm very sorry. But there have been enough people sniffing around here. I can't have a journalist—or a cop, for that matter—getting the word out. I do suppose that once you're dead, I'll read in the papers if you really were a journalist, though."

Before she could say another word, she felt Nick's gun pressing into her back. His other hand went to her side.

"Come on, pretty lady," he said with a chuckle. "Time to take your last ride."

CHAPTER FIFTEEN

The darkness of later evening had started to fall when Nick and Stan guided her back out to the rear lot behind the abandoned store. Ava instantly started scanning her surroundings. She'd heard Nick ask Clay if he wanted them to "take her to the place." She figured that meant they wouldn't kill her right here, out in the open. But she saw no automobiles anywhere nearby. That made her assume that wherever this designated murder location might be, it was likely not very far away.

Nick pushed the gun into her back as he stepped up behind her. He was so close to her that she could feel his breath, hot and nasty, on her neck. "Walk forward and to the right," he said.

She didn't move at first, taking the time to study the directions he was giving. Forward and to the right was going to take her to the side of the plumber's shop—the side located along the edge of a darkened side street.

Nick nudged her again and she walked this time. She did realize that Clay Johnson had ordered them to kill her in a very specific place. It made her wonder what might happen if she refused to move. Would they shoot her right here, out the in the open? She had no idea and she also didn't think it was worth risking it. For the moment, she figured her best bet would be to stick with obeying them. She'd learn a bit more about how they worked, perhaps. Also, she needed to get her gun back. The trick, of course, was to not let them kill her first.

She knew there was a fight coming, but her right hand was still aching and slightly swollen from the business it had taken care of earlier in the day.

They came to the corner of the building and she heard Stan whispering something behind her. She wasn't one hundred percent sure, but she thought it was: "I ain't too sure about killing a broad."

Nick stopped walking suddenly. He reached out and grabbed Ava by the arm, halting her. "What do you mean you ain't sure?"

"I never killed a broad. Seems wrong, you know?"

"Are you for real right now?"

Stan stammered a bit and then said: "I just…I just don't want to do it."

"Then don't. It's not like you ever pull the trigger anyway."

"Hey, that's not true."

"Shut up, Stan. Just come with me and when we get there, you can turn the other way." He followed this up by delivering a hard shove to the center of Ava's back with the barrel of his gun. "Go."

She had taken one step when a sudden noise surprised all of them. It was a loud booming noise that Ava could not quite identify. For a surreal moment, she thought it was thunder—but it was a thunder that was very low to the ground, so close she could feel it rumbling in her head. She did not waste much time trying to figure it out, though. The noise had startled Nick and Stan just as badly as it had startled her and she was not about to lose the chance to quickly get the upper hand in this situation.

Sensing that the gun had been pulled away from her back as the result of Nick's momentary shock, Ava wheeled around and went low, imagining she was ducking a left-handed jab from a boxing opponent. She did this so that if Nick did swivel back around, he'd have to adjust his aim and Ava knew this could prove to be a very valuable half second or so. As it turned out, though, this was an unnecessary precaution. He had turned almost all the way around to see what had made the noise. In doing so, he made himself vulnerable to about a hundred different attacks. Being that he still held the gun, Ava opted for grabbing his right arm and pushing down on his elbow as she pulled back hard on his wrist.

His wrist was pulled back at a painful angle before he knew what was happening. When he turned toward her, Ava brought her knee up into his guts. A gasp of air went racing out of his mouth and when he hunched over, Ava tore the gun away from him and aimed it directly at Stan.

"Give me my gun," she said. "Do it now or I'll take your knees out." She aimed Nick's gun to show she meant business.

Stan nodded nervously and dug her gun out of the inside of his coat. He placed it lightly on the ground and then backed up. Ava narrowed her eyes, wondering why he was being so obedient. Surely he didn't want to look so submissive to a woman in front of his mobster buddy. But then she saw the way his eyes drifted knowingly behind her.

Ava wheeled around just in time to see Nick pulling the small pistol from the waist of his jeans. It was a small model, the sort some dicks hid away with a holster on their ankle. Ava's instinct took over at once; because her instincts were still ingrained in the world of boxing, she did not pull the trigger. Instead, she threw a heavy-handed haymaker that connected squarely with Nick's jaw.

He pulled the trigger less than a second after the impact. There was an alarming moment where Ava was sure she'd been shot even when she saw her punch throw him off and the gun tilted hard to the right. The blast, though, had been so close to her head that it made her ears ring terribly.

With the added impact of the gun clasped in her fist, Nick never stood a chance. He did a simple little stutter-step backwards before crumpling to the ground. Ava then wheeled back around and saw that Stan was going for the gun he'd just now laid on the ground for her.

"Nope. Stand up. I think you and I need—"

She stopped here when she saw movement on the other end of the dark lot, over Stan's shoulder. At first, she feared it was another mobster, maybe drawn out of hiding by the gunshot or the loud thunderous noise beforehand. But the figure was hurrying forward with a clumsy sort of gait that made them not appear threatening at all. When Ava could clearly see the person's face, she rolled her eyes and had a good mind to turn the gun on them instead of Stan.

It was Ronald Amberley. And he looked terrified.

"What the hell are you doing here?" Ava hissed at him.

"Saving your life, apparently."

"What? How do you figure that?"

"That loud noise earlier? That was me. I threw a—"

"I told you not to follow me!"

"Yeah, and you—"

For the second time in less than fifteen seconds, an unexpected sound filled the empty back lot. This time, Ava knew what it was: it was the sound of the loading door opening up. Apparently, Clay Johnson and some of his goons were coming out to see what the banging and the shooting was all about.

Ava knew in that moment that she had a very big and potentially life-or-death decision to make. While it was true that she was a cop and had every reason to be here if there was a distillery on the premises and if these men did in fact have something to do with Millie Newsom's death, the fact remained that these people were *the mob*. If Clay Johnson and Stan and whoever else Clay might bring out of that old building with him could clearly see that they had her outnumbered,

73

they'd kill her. She could stay and fight—and that's what her heart told her to do—but she knew there was a very good chance she'd lose.

So Ava did the one thing she'd never done before over the course of her life.

She ran away from a fight.

"Come on, Amberley," she said, hissing in frustration.

She knelt down to scoop up her precinct firearm and then went running hard to the left, in the opposite direction of the plumber's shop. She figured if that was where Nick and Stan had intended to take her, she wanted to be as far away from it as possible. So she went running across the dark lot as she heard shuffling footsteps coming out of the abandoned building behind her.

"Where ya going, honey pie?" a man's delighted voice asked. Ava had to remind herself that so far, these men thought her name was Vivian Clearwater and she was nothing more than a journalist. She hoped that would help keep her cover for now. More than that, she was pretty sure it meant they wouldn't waste their time in chasing after her.

As she came to the end of the block and crossed the street, mingling back into a very thin stream of pedestrian traffic, she looked back to see if Amberley had kept up. He was a bit slower than her, but he was back there. Ava slowed a bit but did not stop running completely. Within another half a block, Amberley had caught up.

"You created that distraction?" Ava asked. Now that she was removed from the heat of the moment, it was a bit easier to realize how handy that distraction had truly been.

"Yeah." He was panting and red in the face, clearly not accustomed to running so hard.

"Thank you. Now..."

"Nope. We can't stop yet," he said. "They've got goons all over. But my place is just a few streets over. We can hide out there for a while."

Ava wanted to decline the invitation. The last thing she needed was to get more wrapped up in Amberley's shenanigans, especially when he'd already proven how stubborn he could be. Then again, he *was* the closest link she had to Millie Newsom. And the mob night very well be after her, too. So if she could lay low in relative safety for a while, Amberley's home might be the best place.

"Sounds good," she said. "Lead the way."

Amberley crossed the street, and Ava followed. As they slunk away into the darkness, Ava continued checking behind them and peering down every side street and alley, somehow certain that Clay Johnson or one of his men might be waiting there to put a stop to her.

CHAPTER SIXTEEN

During the ten-minute walk to Amberley's apartment, it occurred to Ava that he may be making a play for her. It was a distant thought because Ronald Amberley did not strike her as a typical cake-eater; he was no ladies' man by any stretch of the imagination. It also occurred to her than once she got there, there may be no clear way out if Clay Johnson and his men were patrolling the streets. And she did not relish the thought of staying overnight at the apartment of a man she barely knew.

When they reached his small one-bedroom apartment, it became abundantly clear that he had not asked her back to his place with the hopes of impressing her. He had not tidied up in the amount of time that had passed since she'd broken in. It was still a scattered mess of pads and newspapers. Because she'd already seen it, though, it somehow didn't seem quite as chaotic this time around.

"You're welcome to stay as long as you like," Amberley said. He looked around with a frown on his face, as if realizing for the first time the condition his apartment was in.

"I can't help but wonder if you're used to this...being chased by the mob."

"Not really," he said. "Though there have been a few stories I've chased down with Millie that got people quite mad at me. I only know so much about Clay Johnson's little mob group because they're pretty prominent here."

"Do you think there are dirty cops that look the other way when it comes to Johnson?"

"Oh, for sure. It's one of the many things Millie was looking into. I have no solid proof, but I think it might be what got her killed."

Ava walked to the small, grimy window on the far side of the den. She looked out at the street. She watched several people walk by casually, just out for a late evening stroll. A car went rolling by and as she watched it, she wondered how much longer it would be before the sight of those machines rolling through the city would stop being so fascinating. She could hear the roar of its engine from where she stood, slightly distracting her from her scan of the street. She could see nothing out of the ordinary, no lurking shapes on the corner in search of her.

She thought of what the bartender at the Loose Goose had told her—about how there had been rumors of a nosy female cop they needed to keep their eyes open for. And while Clay Johnson had not come out and said anything specifically, he had certainly been concerned about the presence of a woman with a gun; she wondered if he, too, had heard the rumors of a fabled female detective. Add all of that together with the fact that she was also involved with mob capo August Bonnaci and her life was quickly becoming a very dangerous little web.

"Did you learn anything?" Amberley asked.

Ava snapped her attention away from the window, having only heard the last word of his question. "What was that?"

"You spoke with Clay Johnson, right? I assume that's why those two goons were taking you out with a gun to your back."

"Yes, that's right."

"And did you learn anything from him?"

"He says he didn't know Millie. He claimed he didn't know the identity of the woman that had been shot until someone later told him. He seemed genuinely confused why I was there. I told him I was a journalist, trying to find out what happened to Millie."

"So you believe him?"

"I do. Especially because he was fully prepared to have those men kill me. You'd think in that moment, he would have fessed up. But he seemed to have no idea what I was talking about."

She looked back out onto the street and realized that she was scared to go out. There were just too many unanswered questions, chief among them whether or not Clay Johnson would have men out there looking for her. She supposed she could go out there and hope to hail a cab but doing that in the darkness of night seemed like an unnecessary risk. She'd had trouble with the mob before but now it felt as if half the damn city was on her back.

Then again, if she had to stay with Amberley tonight, would she be any safer in daylight? It sure hadn't helped Millie Newsom at all.

Still, she knew she had to make the right decision here. It was a matter of life or death and if she had to stay here until sunrise…so be it. She could call her father or even Frank, but then what? Neither of them owned an automobile, so it wasn't like they could just come to pick her up.

"I may need to stay here tonight," she said, hating the sound of it. It was far too much like admitting defeat.

"That's fine," he said. "I can put some clean sheets on my bed."

"No, that's okay. I can take one of the chairs in your den."

He nodded and walked over to the chairs, clearing the mess of papers off of both of them. While she watched, that feeling of defeat washed over her even stronger when she realized she was going to have to call her father. She was going to have to tell him that she could not come home tonight and to ask if he could keep an eye on Jeffrey overnight. As this thought occurred to her, though, she became even more confident that staying here was the right choice. If she went back home, there was a very good chance that Johnson and some of his men, or even some of the people involved with the speakeasy at the Loose Goose, would follow her home. That would put Jeffrey and her father both in danger.

She uttered a curse and looked into the den. The one thing aside from newspaper and a pencil stub that she saw was the bulky black shape of Amberley's telephone. Though they were quite common in New York City residences, she was surprised to see that Amberley had one.

"I need to call my father," she said.

"Sure, sure. Help yourself."

She felt a sense of heartbreak as she picked up the receiver. When the operator answered, Ava was nearly whispering when she asked to be connected to her home. She gave the number for her apartment, listened to the operator do her work, and then the line was ringing. After the fifth ring, her father picked up. He sounded gruff and uncertain. She wondered how often the man used a phone in the course of a week...or, hell, even a month. He always bemoaned how he did not like the idea of them.

"Yeah? This is the Gold residence."

"Hey, Dad. It's Ava."

"Oh...hey. Is everything okay?"

"That's a tricky question. I'm currently okay, yes. But it may not be safe for me to come back home tonight. There are some people that might follow me and I don't want them knowing where my family lives."

"Christ, Ava...this sounds serious."

"I know. And to be honest, Dad, I may be overreacting. But it's one of those instances where I'd rather be safe than sorry."

He was quiet for a moment, perhaps understanding what this conversation implied without being explicitly told. He sighed and said, "But you're okay?"

Knowing how to both win her father over *and* make him smile, Ava said: "Yes, I'm fine. My right hands is aching something fierce, though. Had to throw a few punches today."

"Any knockouts?" he asked with a bit of cheer in his voice.

"At least one. Maybe two."

"That's my girl."

"Can I talk to Jeffrey?"

"Sorry, but he's in the shower right now."

"Oh." This hurt her more than she thought it would—needing to be away from her son overnight and not being able to explain it to him herself. "Well, can you tell him what's going on? Just tell him Mommy is playing it safe and needs to stay somewhere else tonight. Give him a kiss and tell him I love him."

"I will. You be careful out there."

"I'm trying," she said with a shaky laugh. "And Dad…I promise it won't always be like this. There's just a lot of groundwork that needs to be laid for this to work…for a woman detective to really make a stand and make sure things are fair. Does that make sense?"

"It does. And I'm damned proud of you. Give 'em hell, okay?"

"I will."

They ended the call and when Ava turned around, she saw that Amberley had busied himself with trying to tidy the place up. He looked rather awkward, having been right behind her while she'd had the conversation with her father.

"Thanks," she said.

"No problem. And you know…I was thinking about it while you were talking. I'm still not convinced Clay Johnson's hands are clean in all of this. I hate to sound biased but if Millie thought her story was centered around him, chances are she was right. And if she was right and he *knew* she was on to him, I think it's obvious."

"That *does* sound biased. I take it you really trusted her."

"I did. Not only in trying to make sure I became a better journalist, but also in just keeping me safe. She knew which parts of town were dangerous, where we'd have issues and where we'd be welcomed warmly. I hope you'll forgive me for saying so, but you remind me a bit of her. I know your story, your speedy journey to the headlines. Like you, Millie had a point to prove and along the way, she swayed a lot of people. More and more people were rooting for her as she became a bigger name with the paper."

"You said you had feelings for her," Ava said.

Amberley shrugged it away. "Yeah, they'd been developing for a while. It was really just an intense infatuation, but yeah, it was there."

"Did she know?"

"Lord no! I would have never told her. I feel like she was just beginning to respect me as a journalist. I wasn't about to ruin that. But she did mean a lot to me and that's why I'm so invested in this case. It's why I chose to follow you today. It's why I'm going against my better judgment and letting you stay here tonight."

"Better judgment?"

"Well, yeah...if the mob is looking for you and I'm harboring you..."

"Oh, okay. I get that, and I appreciate your help."

He chuckled nervously. "Then again, it's probably to my benefit to have a detective with a gun by my side."

They fell into silence for a moment as Amberley continued to clean up his mess. It resulted in a large stack of newspapers standing in the far corner of the den, tucked away behind one of his chairs. She pitched in, though Amberley did his best to cut her off whenever she went to pick something up.

"Do you have any other clues?" he asked her.

She almost said no but then recalled the scrap of paper she had in her pocket. It was hard to believe she'd found it only earlier that day. This day was starting to feel as if it might never end.

"Maybe," she said, digging the scrap of paper out. "I found this taped under Millie's desk. Any idea who George Spotnitz might be?"

He thought about it for a moment, but shook his head. "It doesn't ring a bell."

"The lady sharing an office with Millie didn't recognize it either. But there's an address to go with the name, so I think that's the first place I'm going to visit tomorrow. It was important enough to not only keep, but to keep hidden, too. I suppose it meant *something* to her."

"It could have been one of her sources for this latest story," Amberley offered. "But like I said, she's always been very respectful and secretive of her sources." He sighed deeply and then looked to the kitchen. "I hate to say that I don't have much food to offer you. I can put on some tea, maybe have some crackers and cheese with it?"

"That sounds good, thanks."

She sat down in one of the chairs as Amberley set about getting things together in the kitchen. Ava couldn't help but feel a little distant from the situation, her heart already begging her to change her mind— to chance getting a cab and getting back home to Jeffrey. But with too many people out there aware that she was currently snooping around in mob business, she knew it was far too risky.

What that meant to her was that she was not going to be safe until this case was closed. And she couldn't help but wonder if Captain Minard had known how treacherous it was going to be. Mulling over this, she replayed the day over and over in her head, now more desperate than ever to make sure she'd done all that she could. But as Ronald Amberley made their tea, she kept getting hung up on one thing: the mob had heard of her because of how she'd handled Tony Two during her first case and she was now starting to step on their feet again. She couldn't help but wonder at what point they would decide enough was enough and dispose of her no matter the consequences.

CHAPTER SEVENTEEN

It did not surprise Ava that she slept poorly in the tight-fitting chair in Amberley's living room. There was no room to stretch out and her back was killing her. The little bit of sleep she did manage to get was plagued by strange dreams that kept her shifting uncomfortably in the chair.

In one of the dreams, which was little more than a fragment, she was back out on the street where Millie Newsom had been killed. She was canvassing the street with a partner that she knew well—a partner she had lived with and loved for nearly a decade before he'd been killed in the line of duty. Clarence walked alongside her, studying the streets along with her. He then turned his eyes to her and when they locked eyes, she could recall the intensity of his stare even while she slept.

"This case is too difficult," he said. "Better leave it to those better equipped. You go on home and stay safe. Be a good mom and take care of our kid."

"But I can do this," Ava argued. "There's got to be an answer somewhere."

As he considered his answer Ava watched as two people came around the corner behind him. They walked right by the newsstand Ava had seen in the real, waking world, and began to fight. One pulled a knife and slashed the other directly across the throat.

"Answers aren't always going to be right in front of you, never as simple and as direct as spilled blood," Clarence said. "You have to try harder."

"But there's so much trouble out there waiting for me. I'm afraid I've gotten in too deep."

"Of course you have," he said. "That's why you just need to quit. You were never cut out for this, Ava. I love you, but this is so much harder than you're capable of handling."

As he spoke to her, the blood from the fallen man behind them seeped down the street. It collected around her shoes and both she and Clarence watched it pool around her heels, but said nothing.

"It's okay," Clarence said. "Quit. Leave it for others. Leave it for the capable men on the force."

More blood pooled around her feet and this time when she looked back to the fallen body, it was Millie Newsom. It was Millie as she'd seen her on the coroner's table, only her pale lips were drawn back in a smile. She parted them and her tongue moved. She formed a single word that came out in a stagnant breath that Ava could clearly smell, despite the distance.

"Quit..."

Ava awoke with a jerk, nearly falling right out of Ronald Amberley's chair. She sat up and looked around the room. Her tired, swirling mind was actively looking for Clarence to be there for a moment. Ave closed her eyes and shook her head, as if to dislodge the nonsense. Jittery and feeling slightly outside of her own head, she got out of the chair and walked into the kitchen. She rummaged through Amberley's mostly-empty cabinets until she found a glass. She filled it with water from the tap and drank it slowly as she stood in the dark and unfamiliar kitchen.

She'd had numerous dreams about Clarence since he'd passed away, but this one had been different. This one had her shaken. Not quite aware of what she was doing, Ava walked over to the phone. She toyed with the idea of calling her father, just to hear Jeffrey's voice, but she had no idea what time it was. With no watch on her wrist and no visible clock anywhere in Amberley's apartment, she could only guess at the time and she assumed it was well after midnight.

Still, she picked up the receiver and before she knew it, the operator was asking her which line she'd like to be connected to. She gave a number she'd only called once before, a number she was rather surprised she could remember without any problem. The operator did her job and then the other line began to ring in her ear.

After four rings, Ava nearly hung up. She knew this might be a bad idea, that she might be crossing a line. But by the time this thought had fully developed, the other line was answered.

"Hello?" Frank said. She had very clearly woken him up with her call. His voice was ragged, tired, and confused.

"I'm so sorry," Ava said. "I know it's late."

"Ava?"

"Yeah. Let's pretend I never called. I'll let you go back to sl—"

"No, no, it's okay." His voice grew clearer, almost bright now. "It *is* late, but I'm glad to hear from you. Are you okay?"

"I've been better. I'm still in Brooklyn, staying in a journalist's apartment."

"Why? Do you need a cab? Need me to—"

"No, nothing like that." She kept her voice soft, as to not wake up Amberley, who was in the bedroom with the door closed. "I may have made some mobsters very angry today."

"Jesus, Ava…"

"You ever heard of Clay Johnson?"

He thought about it for a moment before answering: "No, I don't think so. Are you sure you're okay?"

"Yeah. I just didn't think it was smart to venture back home at night. Even if I made it safely, I didn't want to take the chance of some of these creeps following me home and knowing where my family lives." She nearly slipped up and mentioned the already-existing trouble she had with another arm of the mob, but caught herself just in time.

"I can sneak over to Brooklyn tomorrow if you need me to," Frank said. "Minard would never even know."

"No. I don't want to risk it."

"Let me guess. You just want to solve the case as quickly as possible so that you can rub Minard's face in it."

"No, I won't be rubbing anything. I'm hoping my work will speak for itself."

"Well, continuing to piss of the mob will certainly get your name out there, that's for sure." He paused here and then, his voice still alert, asked: "Did you call me just to tell me about your day? Are you sure you're okay?"

"Yes. I just feel…I don't know. *Lonely* isn't quite the word. But I wanted to speak with Jeffrey or my dad. It's the first night I've spent away from them in a very long time and the first *ever* since Clarence passed away. I wanted to speak to someone familiar and I figure instead of waking them up…"

"That you'd wake *me* up."

"Exactly." Then, after some consideration, she added: "Sorry."

"It's okay."

"I'll take your word for it. But I *am* going to get off of here. It's not even my phone and I really should try to get some sleep."

"This journalist…is it a man or a woman."

"A man. But he's harmless. Oh…or are you jealous?"

"Hell yes, I'm jealous," he said with a laugh.

"Goodnight, Frank."

"G'night."

Ava ended the call, placing the receiver softly back onto its cradle. She ventured back over to the chair, certain that it would be impossible go back to sleep. To her surprise, she drifted off quickly and did not wake up until the first glow of morning light came through Ronald Amberley's windows and set upon her face.

CHAPTER EIGHTEEN

Ava woke up with a severe pain in her neck and a right leg tingling with pins and needles, but she felt surprisingly refreshed. The morning light spilling in through the window told her that it was likely somewhere just beyond six in the morning. She got out of the chair and walked back into Amberley's kitchen. Apparently, he was not an early riser, as he was nowhere to be seen and the bedroom door was still closed.

Ava searched his kitchen, hoping to find some coffee, but there was none. She settled for another cup of tea and sat with it at Amberley's kitchen table. She noticed that Amberley had set Millie's notebook down on the counter, so she had a look through it as she sipped from her tea. She looked for anything that might resemble a clue, even some of the things that were scratched out. But in the longhand form and in very brief statements and sentences that read almost like code, she could find nothing.

She then picked up one of the nubs of pencil and an old newspaper. She thought through what she knew of the Millie Newsom case and made a list, trying to make sense of it by viewing it from a different angle. She wrote down the names of everyone involved so far, including the name of the Loose Goose, where she'd been attacked at the speakeasy, and the Duck Pond, which she was in agreement with the rumors as being a code name for a distillery. She even took a shot and wrote down Tony Two's name, wondering if his arm of the mob might have a hand to play in all of this.

But even if he did, did it matter? In the end, Ava's mind kept going back to the reaction she'd gotten out of Clay Johnson when she mentioned Millie Newsom. While she knew it was foolish to take a mafioso's word at face value, she was also a decent judge of when someone was being dishonest. Her gut told her that Johnson had been just as confused by Millie's death as she was.

Her near certainty of this raised another question. It was a question she'd briefly considered yesterday but now seemed to loom much larger after her encounter with Johnson.

What if the mob had absolutely nothing at all to do with Millie's death? What if she'd been wasting her time going after the mob? After all, even Amberley had suggested dirty cops might also be in the mix. Maybe she was being a bit presumptive to assume the two were automatically connected.

As she started to properly give this some thought, she heard the bedroom door open. Amberley had already gotten dressed for the day, wearing a basic white shirt and a pair of pants that might last a few more washes before they fell apart. One look at his head told her that he'd made no attempt to straighten up his hair yet, though.

"Sorry," Ava said, tapping at her teacup. "I sort of made myself at home."

"I'm glad you did. Sorry I don't have much in the way of breakfast. I usually just grab a biscuit and jam down at the diner on the corner."

"I won't lie...that sounds pretty good." She kept to herself that a shower and a toothbrush also sounded good. These were not things she'd thought about the night before, though. "Would you mind if I freshened up as best as I can before I head back out?"

"Sure. The bathroom is attached to my room." He set about making his own cup of tea and then asked, "Where are you heading first today?"

"I'm going to look into George Spotnitz. I want to find out why she had his name hidden."

He nodded, though it was clear the idea made him uncomfortable. She wasn't sure if it was because he didn't like the idea of Millie keeping a secret about another man or if he feared it might lead Ava away from the mob connection he seemed to be stuck on. He said nothing else as Ava finished her tea and excused herself to the restroom.

She'd expected Amberley's bedroom to be in the same state as she'd found it yesterday, but it was surprisingly clean. The bed had already been made and though there was no real furniture aside from the bed, he had clothes hanging on racks from a pole that ran the length of the room. She found the bathroom in an equally clean state, which was a relief. She'd lived with a man for almost a decade and knew how gross they could be when it came to keeping a bathroom. Her father's short stay at her apartment so far was only proving her theory that men forgot how to clean up after themselves in the bathroom. Ronald Amberley, though, seemed to be an exception.

She found a tube of Colgate dental ribbon cream and quirted some out on her finger. She did her best to brush her teeth this way and then spent a few moments doing her best to wipe down the key areas of her body. Amberley had a shower, of course, but she was not comfortable with the idea of stripping down naked in a man's apartment.

When she rejoined him in the kitchen five minutes later, Amberley was putting his shoes on. "If we can get down to the diner in the next few minutes, the biscuits will have just come out of the oven, nice and fresh. My treat."

"You don't have to do that," Ava said.

"But I insist. Plus, I feel like if we walk out together, anyone who might be sniffing around for you might either not see you or think twice about doing anything. Safety in numbers and all that."

"Okay. But I need you to understand that we are parting ways after that. I meant what I said yesterday, but it didn't seem to sink in: you can't follow me around. You may be a promising journalist, but you're no detective. Hell, I'm not even sure I have *my* detective feet properly under me just yet."

"But I know people," he argued. "I can help. I can maybe even help hook you up with people that know a great deal about the mob. No one knew Millie better than I did. I think I could really be useful."

She knew he had a point but there was no way she could work effectively with a civilian following her around. An idea slowly came to her. She had no idea if he would accept it, but she figured it could actually work to both their advantages.

"There's no way I can have you with me as a partner. And I would greatly appreciate it if you didn't sneak around like you did yesterday and tail me. But you're right: I think you *could* help. I want you to look through that notebook. I want you to study it, to really dig deep from cover to cover. Anything that you think might remotely be linked to why she might have died or someone she may not have trusted…I need to know things like that. For now, that's the only way I can allow you to help."

Amberley looked to the notebook and sighed. "That's just the thing, Detective Gold. I've looked through that thing at least four times since she died."

"Yes, but was it as a way to remember her or was it with a critical eye?"

A subtle determination crept into his face as he continued to stare at the book. "Good point. Yeah, I can do that. But will you at least keep me posted if you find anything?"

"Absolutely. As a matter of fact, you'll be the first person I notify."

"Okay."

She headed for the door and turned back to him with a smile. "I suppose I *can* allow you to still come with me to buy me jam and biscuits. I may be stubborn and something of a loner, but a girl's got to eat."

CHAPTER NINETEEN

Several cups of coffee had accompanied the biscuits and jam. The stiffness was coming out of her neck and by the time she left the diner, it was almost as if she hadn't spent the night sleeping uncomfortably in a small chair. She wanted to immediately go out looking for Spotnitz, assuming that going by his address before eight in the morning would allow her to speak with him before he left his home for the day. But at the same time, she knew the responsible thing to do would be to visit the precinct to update Skinner.

She didn't like the idea of starting her day back in that hostile precinct, but she made herself do it. When she entered the building, the large clock on the wall above the large bullpen told her that it was 7:20. She wondered if Skinner was even the type of chief to come in at such an hour. The bullpen was mostly empty, as the night shift and day shift were currently in the process of swapping roles. She could even smell the light fragrance of an industrial cleaner the cleaning crew had used during the night.

Just to follow protocol, she walked back to Skinner's office and knocked. She was not expecting an answer, so when he hollered out "Yeah?" right away, she was shocked. Before opening the door, she did notice that he sounded like he was in a much better mood than he had been yesterday.

She entered his office and couldn't help but enjoy the look of shock and confusion on his face when he saw her.

"Oh, Gold! Good morning. Wasn't expecting to see you today. I thought you'd be back in Manhattan by now."

"No sir," she said, confused and irritated all at once. "I still haven't closed the case."

"The case?" He looked genuinely confused for a moment, almost in a panic. He then clapped his hands together and gave an enthusiastic nod. "Oh, right, right. The Millie Newsom case. What have you got?"

She took a moment before she spoke, afraid her anger would take over. The bastard had all but forgotten why she was even here. More than that, he'd been surprised she hadn't already headed back home—

as if she were nothing more than some sappy dame who would run back home, licking her wounds.

"Well, I spoke at length to the man that had been partnered with her at the paper as an apprentice of sorts. He believed without a doubt that someone from the mob had something to do with her being killed. He had no hard evidence, though, and there was nothing to be found in Millie's notebook, which he currently has in his possession. So I followed some leads and ended up coming across a speakeasy in the back room of a place called The Loose Goose."

She paused here, expecting a reaction. Perhaps he'd even thank her for finding such a place and bringing it to his attention. But no...she got nothing. Undeterred, she went on.

"Another trail led me to investigate a rumor of something known as the Duck Pond—a place many believe to be a distillery. Now, while I never saw an actual distillery, I did have a run-in with the man who was on the street when Millie was killed. He just happens to be a mafioso named Clay Johnson."

"Hold on," Skinner said, suddenly very interested. "You spoke to Johnson?"

"Yes, sir."

"You spoke to him, face-to-face, and asked about his possible involvement in the death of a journalist?"

"Yes, sir. And he nearly had some of his goons knock me off."

"By God, Gold. I'm not sure if you're incredibly brave or just plain stupid."

"Excuse me?"

"You're telling me that the simple murder investigation of a journalist somehow led you to being in a meeting with Clay Johnson and sniffing around a rumored distillery?"

"Yes, sir." She found it very hard to remain cordial and polite, forcing herself to get the *sir* out. "I went where the leads were telling me to go."

"And did it get you any closer to finding the killer?"

It was a fair question, but she resented the mocking tone he used. But really, she expected nothing more. The only reason Minard tolerated her back on her home turf was because he'd known Clarence. And maybe—*just maybe*—because he was starting to see that she was pretty damned good at this job. Of course, Captain Skinner had seen none of that.

"No, it did not."

"But it nearly got you killed, by your own admission. And wouldn't that be a hell of a note. The up-and-coming celebrity broad detective Ava Gold is sent to Brooklyn to help with a case and then dies on my watch."

"Your *watch*, sir? It seemed you barely even knew I was still here."

Skinner got up out of his seat so fast that she thought his large, rotund frame might knock the desk over. He leveled a fat finger at her and said, "You watch your tone. And get the hell out of my building. Get out there on the street and do what you came here to do. Find that poor woman's killer!"

Ava obeyed at once. She did not out of respect for Skinner or his position, but mainly because she did not trust herself to keep her mouth shut. She knew her last comment had crossed a line that most men were not used to women crossing, no matter their status. So she pushed the door open and crossed quickly through the bullpen and to the front door. Fortunately, there still weren't many day shift cops in just yet so she was able to make it back out to the street without making any further scenes.

However, as she soon as she made it down the stairs of the precinct and to the sidewalk, someone called her name from the right. It was a police officer, and when he called her he did so quietly. It was clear he wanted no one else to hear. He was a bit on the younger side, clean shaven and with a scrawny build that made his policeman's uniform appear far too large on him.

"Detective Gold?"

She was expecting more ridicule or discouraging remarks like she'd received yesterday, but this man surprised her. He stepped closer to her and then looked back over his shoulders to make sure no one was paying attention to them.

"A quick note about your case. You can't—"

"And what exactly do you know about my case?" she interrupted.

He shook his head and gave her a worried expression. "Oh, it doesn't matter what case you're working on. You're a woman and I know you're here from some other precinct in Manhattan. That means you don't really know how things work here. So just let me tell you…be careful. Be *very* careful about how deep you dig."

"And what do I need to be careful about?"

He was already stating up the stairs to the front door now, apparently not wanting to take the chance of someone seeing him speak with her. "Just watch your back," he added quickly. "It would be far too easy for you to get hurt, or worse."

"Is that a warning or a threat?"

The look he fired her way was the same one of scorn and anger she'd seen so many times from men who thought it was out of line to be questioned in such a way by a woman. As he fumbled for an answer, Ava took note of the name on the pin above his pocket: Banner.

"Take it how you want," he said. And the way he looked at her told her all she needed to know. He had never intended to give her a fair warning. He was not the friendly and helpful cop he'd at first presented himself to be. Just like all of the others, he was trying to get in her head, trying to sabotage her.

She watched him enter the station, committing the last name of Banner to mind. Then, with no intention of letting yet another man slow her down, Ava walked a few blocks over where she attempted to hail a cab. She had the scrap of paper from beneath Millie's desk clutched in her hand, still hoping to meet with George Spotnitz before the day got away from her.

CHAPTER TWENTY

When she stepped out of the cab on Holloway Street just under fifteen minutes later, she asked the driver for the time. When he told her it was five minutes after eight, Ava feared she may have missed George Spotnitz. Most people with typical jobs were out and about by eight in the morning. If that were the case here, she'd likely spend most of her day trying to figure out where Spotnitz worked. Hoping he may still be home, she hurried to the door of the small house and knocked on the door.

As she looked around from the doorstop, she supposed George Spotnitz must be doing very well for himself. It was a small house, but it was a house all the same. Holloway Street appeared to be dominated by this exact same style of house for a good stretch of real estate. She knocked once more when there was no answer, fully prepared to consider this visit a loss. But within a few seconds of this second knock, she heard the locks on the other side of the door being disengaged.

The door opened just a few inches and a tall man peered out at her. He looked tired, as if she may have just stirred him awake. "Yes? Can I help you?"

She showed her badge, which he squinted at, and introduced herself. "I'm Detective Ava Gold. Are you George Spotnitz?"

"I am," he said. He sounded curious more than concerned. And was waking up quite fast after discovering a detective at his door.

"Mr. Spotnitz, I'm looking into the death of Millie Newsom. Does that name a ring a bell for you?"

"It does," he said. She could see pain in his eyes as he wrestled back emotion at the mention of her name. "It's a very loud bell, in fact."

"I assume you've heard about what happened?"

"Yes," he said, again seeming to struggle.

"I'd like to ask you a few questions."

"Of course. But I've just gotten out of bed. Would you allow me a few minutes to get properly dressed?"

"Of course."

He shut the door, but not all the way, perhaps letting her know he had nothing to hide. Still, out of respect, she remained on the front stoop until he came back to the door two minutes later. He'd thrown on a pair of slacks, an undershirt, and a respectable-looking sportscoat. He'd not put shoes on yet, so his bare feet made the ensemble rather funny.

He led her into his living room, a modestly furnished room that was about the size of Ronald Amberley's entire apartment. "Would you like me to put some coffee on?" he asked politely.

"No thank you." She studied him a bit as they settled into their respective seats—Ava taking a plain armchair while Spotnitz sat on a small couch. She guessed him to be in his late twenties. A moustache covered his upper lip but the remainder of his face was cleanly shaved. He was quite handsome in an unsuspecting way, and she could already tell that his charm and skill with polite conversation likely made up for anything a woman might consider him lacking in appearance.

"Forgive me for asking," Spotnitz said, "but how did you know to come see me?"

Ava showed him the small piece of paper she'd removed from beneath Millie's desk. "This was hidden under her desk. It's clear that she wanted to keep it, but also keep it hidden. So it makes me think you may be my best lead in terms of finding her killer because so far, it's been a very bumpy road."

"Well, sadly, I can tell you nothing about who might have killed her. As you might imagine, she made quite a few enemies with her job. But all the same, she never told me about feeling afraid or threatened."

"How did you know her?" Ava asked. "What was the scope of your relationship?"

A sad smile crossed his face as he looked for the right words. "She came to me about a year ago for some help with researching a story on the sewer situation in eastern Brooklyn. Ever since then, I've sort of been a contact for her. I'm assuming she had that slip of paper because I moved recently and, as smart as she was, she was never good with memorizing addresses or numbers."

"And why would she come to you for information? What sort of contact were you?"

"I'm something of a history scholar. I know how pretentious that sounds, but it's the truth. I've written two books about the growth and popularity of New York City, one about Abraham Lincoln's presidency, and I'm currently working on one about the politics of the

Boston Tea Party. The first time she came to me for help, she stated that she'd read my first book on New York several times and asked if I would be of some assistance."

The success of his books explained how he was able to own such a nice house at such a young age. It made her wonder what sort of enemies Spotnitz might have made during his climb to success.

"So it was a professional relationship?"

Spotnitz frowned at the question and shifted in his seat. "We became very good friends but we kept it secret. She did not want people knowing that she had me helping her with research. She wanted people to think she was perfectly fine on her own."

"Did she pay you for this service?"

"She offered to a few times but I never let her. She was a great journalist. Her instincts were incredible. She could smell a story from a mile away and my God, the woman was amazing at knowing when someone was lying to her."

"When was the last time you spoke with her?" She asked this question while keeping note of the way he had shifted a bit when she'd asked if it had only been a professional relationship.

"The day before she died," he answered.

"Did she mention anything about the current story she was working on?"

"Not in any great detail. She just said that she wasn't looking forward to speaking to a bunch of cops. She said she had some interviews to conduct with them, but wouldn't tell me why." He laughed for a second at this, but there was no humor in it. All she could hear was pain. "Even as a very good friend, she remained secretive about her stories. I would tease her sometimes about how it was foolish to think I'd steal her ideas, but that's just the way she was."

"Her secrecy around her stories seems to be a common theme," Ava said. "Do you know why?"

"Well, it's obvious, isn't it? She didn't want a male reporter swiping up any story ideas or leads. I'm sure you know all about that, right? I know ladies have equal rights now but that still hasn't changed the male mindset. And Millie was very aware of that."

"Do you have *any* idea of what she was working on when she was shot?"

"No. I'm sorry."

Ava was surprised to see a tear slip out of the corner of his eye. It made her want to press a bit more, to ask one more time if there was nothing else going on between them.

"I'm sorry," he said. "She was a dear friend and this is the first I've spoken about it at length with anyone. It's…well, it's harder than I expected it to be. Do you mind if we cut this short? You're welcome to come back later, but for right now…I just don't know if I can."

"Yes, of course," she said. It felt like a defeat, coming here to this secretive address and finding out very little. She got to her feet and started toward the door when her eyes drifted to the mantel over the small fireplace.

There were two decorative vases and two photographs, each picture propped up against a vase. One of the photos was of an older woman, perhaps in her fifties—maybe Spotnitz's mother. The other, though, was of a young woman. Ava almost didn't recognize her at first because of the smile; it was a stark contrast to the face she'd seen on the coroner's table. It was a candid shot, the sort of picture the photographer likely caught when they weren't expecting it. In fact, it didn't look like Millie knew the picture was being taken at all. She couldn't help but wonder if Spotnitz had been the photographer.

"This is her?" Ava asked, looking at the picture.

With an almost guilty tone to his voice, Spotnitz said, "Yes, that's her."

Ava stepped closer to the picture. She was quite sure it wasn't just her; anyone who did not know Spotnitz or Millie Newsom would have likely seen the picture and assumed Millie was a sister or some other family member. In the picture, she looked so happy, caught mid-laugh in a candid and vulnerable state—the kind of state only someone very close to them would be able to capture.

"Mr. Spotnitz," she said. "I'd really like to know everything I could about her."

He started slowly nodding right away. He wiped a few tears away and picked the picture up, looking at it with an intense longing.

"It got romantic after about three months. We never committed to one another or anything like that, but by all intents and purposes, we were a couple. We were frequently intimate but rarely stayed at the other's place. That made it feel a little too real."

"And were you together up until her death?"

"No. Whatever it was we had, it only last three or four months. We realized that we got along much better when we were just friends."

97

"Did it end on good terms?"

Spotnitz placed the picture back in its place and seemed to drift away into his own internal thoughts for a moment. "I suppose so. Things were a little strained between us for a month or so, but we missed each other. We both admitted it. For her, it was like pulling teeth. She didn't like showing vulnerability."

Ava listened closely, but she was hung up on two things. First of all, she wasn't sure why he would have initially lied about a relationship with Millie if it was as innocent as he was saying it had been. And second, something about the picture didn't sit right with her. It was a good picture of Millie, but it had the look and angle of a picture that had been taken in secret. It made her wonder if Spotnitz might have been following her in secret from time to time.

"Mr. Spotnitz, do you own a gun?"

The question surprised both of them—Ava by how blunt it had come out and Spotnitz by the out-of-the-blue nature of the inquiry.

"I'm not sure what that has to do with anything."

"Hopefully nothing. But you're going to make my day a lot easier if you can just answer the question."

It was clear that he did not want to give her an answer. But she watched as a dull realization crossed his face, understanding that his reluctance to answer was very likely all the answer she needed.

"Yes, I have a gun. A simple little revolver."

"Can I see it?"

She didn't see any real fear in his eyes, but a great deal of uncertainty. "Yeah, it's stored away, though."

She left the living room area and entered the hallway. Ava followed him down the hall. It was a beautiful, yet small house. The wooden floors didn't show many signs of wear, and the walls were adorned with simple art prints. Spotnitz stopped at a closet at the end of the hallway. He opened it to reveal several suits hanging up and a few pairs of shoes on the floor. There was a small shelf above the clothes, stacked with reams of paper and an old typewriter. He removed a small showbox from beside the typewriter and took it out. When he handed the box over to her, she saw some nerves for the first time. She thought she saw some trembling in his arm and worry in his eyes.

She opened the shoebox and found a small revolver. She wasn't quite sure of the make or brand, but Clarence had once owned one similar to it. She was quite sure her father owned one similar in appearance as well.

"When was the last time you fired the gun?" Ava asked.

Again, Spotnitz did not answer right away. When he finally did speak, it was not with an answer to her question. "I can't help but feel that you're treating me as a suspect."

"With all due respect," Ava said, "I have to treat everyone as a suspect until they are proven innocent."

She could tell that George Spotnitz was quickly losing his patience. Still, he finally answered her. "I've only fired that gun twice. Once was during a drunken bachelor party for a friend where we shot glass bottles in an alleyway. The second and last time was about two months ago when a drunken teenager attempted to break into my house."

"Did you *shoot* this teenager?"

"No. Just fired up into the air to scare him off."

Ava checked the chamber and found two rounds missing. If the stories he'd just told were true, the two missing rounds could mean nothing. Millie's report said there had only been one shot fired. None of it lined up.

"I can quite easily rule myself out as being Millie's killer," Spotnitz said. "If that truly is what you're trying to figure out."

She could see that she'd angered him, but there was a deep-seated hurt there as well. Perhaps he truly had felt strongly for her and was offended by the notion that someone might think he'd kill her.

"And how's that?"

"I had a very long and tiresome meeting with my publisher that afternoon. It started at lunch and I didn't get home until well after five o'clock. I learned about her death around eight that night, when a mutual friend informed me. I can give you at least three names that can verify that I was in a conference room for that entire afternoon."

It was a brave play if he was lying...which made her sure he wasn't. She nodded and there was an unspoken understanding between them in that moment. She knew he was innocent and he knew she believed him.

"I'm very sorry for your loss," she said. "But please know that if anything in this case does point back to you, I'm going to take you up on getting those names."

"Why wait?" he said, and when he spoke those two words, she could tell that he was on the verge of breaking down into an uncontrollable crying fit. He reached into the coat pocket of one of the coats in the closet and pulled out a folded sheet of paper. Written on it

99

were a series of notes with a *Goldstein Publishers* letterhead at the top. There were two names under the letterhead, along with an address.

"I kept it because of the editorial notes they provided…but I haven't even thought about them yet."

"Thank you," Ava said, taking the paper. "I'll return the notes to you when the case is over. And please, if you think of anything else…"

He nodded, but didn't dare speak. She could practically feel the grief coming off of him now. He led her to the door quickly, clearly not wanting her to see him break down into tears. Yet even when she was outside and George Spotnitz's door was closed behind her, she heard it when it began. It was a sound that told Ava one more thing about Spotnitz: whether he wanted to admit it or not, he'd been in love with Millie Newsom. Thinking of Ronald Amberley, she thought it seemed to be going around.

With her last promising lead having come to nothing, Ava once again found herself unsure of where to go next. She knew it was still rather early but she thought she may go back to Amberley's apartment to see if he'd had any luck with Millie's notebook. She truly hoped he had because if not, this case was going to get the best of her.

CHAPTER TWENTY ONE

On her way back to Amberley's, she stopped by the diner he'd treated her to breakfast and grabbed two coffees. She carried them to his apartment and he seemed pleased to have it when he greeted her at the door.

"You're back a lot sooner than I thought you'd be," Amberley said. "I won't lie, when I heard that knock at the door, I almost hid again."

"Are you that scared of dirty cops? Did Millie piss off *that* many people?"

"She did," he said with a chuckle. "But after last night, I'm concerned about the mob, too. Clay Johnson doesn't tend to let bygones be bygones. Just because the sun is up doesn't mean you can let *your* guard down, either."

"I'm being careful."

"And quick, apparently. No luck with this Spotnitz character?"

"Oh, I've already spoken with him."

"Oh yeah? Who was it, exactly?"

"Someone Millie used as a source. And I can't tell you anything more than that. You've said yourself she was very secretive about that sort of thing."

"And he knew nothing?"

"No. Just about how good she was at her job."

Amberley nodded, and she was relieved when he didn't ask anything else about Spotnitz. She did not enjoy lying, but she had no intentions of telling Amberley that one of the reasons Millie may not have been interested in him was because she'd been spending a lot of time with Spotnitz.

"How about you?" she asked as she sat down to the table with her coffee. "Were you able to decipher anything else out of the notebook?"

"Maybe. It might be a bit of a stretch, but definitely worth a gander." He took the notebook off of the kitchen counter and plopped it down on the kitchen table. He flipped through a few pages and pointed to a few scribbled notes near the final page she'd written. Ava recalled the page quite well...a list of some kind that Millie had very thoroughly scratched out. Along the margins, though, there were a few other names. Some of these had been crossed out as well, but there was one that seemed to have been circled and then crossed out as almost an afterthought.

"This name," Amberley said. "All I can tell for sure right here is that it was circled at one time…unlike any other name on the list. I can't tell for sure what it is. All I can see is that it ends in an E-R."

Ava eyed the name, but the E-R was also all she could see. Curious, she turned the paper over to the other side. There were scribblings on the back, too, but none in the margins. It was still very hard to see, but the indentations of the pencil that had been used to make the notes were easier to follow. The name that ended in E-R was *Banner*.

"Banner," she said.

"Is that a familiar name to you?"

"Not until this morning. I had a run-in with a cop named Banner. He tried to warn me about digging too deep."

"Well, if it *is* the same Banner and he knew Millie was on to him, he would surely have a reason to not want you digging too deep."

Ava sipped from her coffee and thought about it for a moment. At first, Banner had seemed almost polite and helpful. But when she'd not cowered when he'd shifted to an almost ominous approach, Banner had then tried a more direct approach. He'd not *quite* threatened her, but the polite polish he'd shown at first had been gone. Looking back on it, it was almost as if he'd been testing the waters, trying to find out how much she knew and how much resolve she had to really sink her teeth into the case.

"Do you recall the name ever coming up?" Ava asked.

"I don't think so. But then again, I don't think she ever named one specific person when she was dealing with mobsters or potential dirty cops. She was always very careful not to put a name out there unless she knew for sure."

"Okay, but do you think the inclusion of his name at least makes it seem likely that she was looking into Banner as being a dirty cop?"

"I'd say it's a safe bet. Actually, with it being circled, I'd say it's a *very* safe bet."

Ava thought it through before just getting to her feet and heading out. Even if she were familiar with the 77th precinct and the men who worked there, she couldn't just start accusing cops. That would be a risky move to make even if she were a man.

"If you want, I can see if there are any of her old contacts that know anything about him," Amberley said.

"Not yet. Honestly, I still just want you to stay put. If you're linked directly to Millie, they'll come after you. It'll be even worse if they think you're working with me. At this point, I have at least two power figures with reason to want me silenced."

"Yes, I know. I've been there both times."

She grinned at him and nodded. "See? You're practically proving my point. You stay put."

"And what about you? Where are you going?"

She got up from the table, still holding her coffee. "It looks like I'm heading back to the precinct to see if there really are any dirty cops."

CHAPTER TWENTY TWO

Frank often wondered if he could have been an accountant in another life. He didn't particularly enjoy working with numbers, but he liked the stories numbers could tell. One of his favorite things to do after a long day at work was to grab a newspaper and look at the box scores of the baseball games. Right there, just a series of numbers in boxes, telling their story of a three-hour span of time. The same was true whenever he worked a case that had him looking at the financial records of a suspect or victim. The state of their financial affairs often told him more about their way of life than most loved ones could.

He found himself looking into that sort of thing on the second morning Ava was working out of the 77th precinct. He had the financial record and bank statements of Victor D'Amour on his desk, and it was a thick stack indeed. The tricky part was that if you looked at the current balances, one might get the idea that D'Amour had been living an exceptional life. At the time of his death, he'd had nearly seven hundred thousand dollars in the bank, and another thirty thousand wrapped up in bonds.

But, just like those baseball box scores, the numbers and entries that led up to those impressive numbers told a bit of a different story. Buried in the papers and records of D'Amour's financial affairs was evidence that all of the money he had and all the money he had incoming for the next several months was already spent. He owed it to land developers, stockbrokers, and several unnamed sources that Frank assumed were the mob or some form of illegal gambling. If D'Amour were to pay off every dollar he owed, he'd be more than fifteen thousand dollars in debt.

But those same records showed that D'Amour had no intention of paying anyone off. He was still spending money on elaborate things like trips to Europe, a Ford Model A automobile, and several very expensive dresses for his fourteen-year-old daughter.

And another untold story that came not in the form of numbers, but an autopsy report: the angle and proximity of the gunshot wound suggested one of two things. Either D'Amour's killer was very short—as in, less than five feet tall—and angled the gun upward—or the wound had been self-inflicted. Looking at the financial records and knowing the sort of proud man D'Amour was rumored to be, the facts of the matter seemed pretty clear to Frank.

There was only one real question remaining, and that was what had happened to the gun. If D'Amour had truly killed himself right in front of his apartment, without bothering to go inside, the gun he'd used to do it should have been right there by his body. But there had been no gun at the scene.

It was a puzzle for sure, but Frank had learned to never take the first overall glimpse of a crime scene at face value when there was a wealthy victim involved. He thought of D'Amour's wife, a timid younger woman, and what her train of thought might look like if she came home and discovered her husband dead on the floor in front of their apartment. She'd not been very talkative when he'd questioned her and at the time, he'd chalked it up to nothing more than trauma and loss.

But now he wondered if there was something else. Maybe there was something she was hiding.

Frank wasn't just grasping at straws here either. As he'd been asking around about other people who knew Victor D'Amour, he'd come to understand that over the last six to eight months, there had been a lot of deaths in their field. Not just deaths, but suicides. Just a little over a month ago, some bruno had taken a leap from the top of the fifteen-story building he'd worked at. In his pocket, there'd been a note that read: *Money isn't worth this and truth be told, trouble is coming.*

With the message of that note in mind, Frank stood up from his desk and walked to the back of the bullpen. He'd never quite understood why, but working a case that involved suicides always unnerved him. And with this one, his research had shown him that in those six to eight months where so many financial-types had died, fourteen were confirmed suicides. Apparently, things weren't going so well in the financial sector.

As he made his way into the breakroom and poured a cup of coffee, he thought of Delia D'Amour, coming home and finding her husband dead in front of their door. A man who had cared and provided for her for so long, a man who had earned quite a respectable reputation over the years. Then he wondered what she might do if she saw a gun lying by the body. It would be simple to put the pieces together and figure out that he'd taken his own life. But in that moment, what would a woman like Delia D'Amour do? In her loss, sorrow, and maybe even anger at the idea that her cowardly husband had taken his own life, would she think of herself? Would she think of the legacy her husband would leave behind?

Would she pick up that gun and hide it, unaware of what the autopsy reports would suggest several days later?

Frank wished Ava were there to discuss it all with him. His instincts told him that he had uncovered the path he needed to travel, but he needed validation. After all, approaching a recent widow and accusing her of hiding evidence that her husband had committed suicide was not going to be easy. And dear God, if he was *wrong*, what sort of monster would he appear to be?

"But I'm not wrong," he told himself.

"What's that?"

Frank had barely even noticed there was another officer in the breakroom, nibbling on crackers at the small table. It was a bit embarrassing, being found talking to yourself. But he shrugged it off and said, "Ah, nothing. Thinking out loud." Which was really the truth.

Coffee finished, Frank went back to his desk. He did not sit down, though. If he sat down, he knew he would procrastinate. So, still standing, he checked the autopsy report once more. He looked to the numbers he'd viewed several times, the number of men in the financial sector who had offed themselves recently.

And he thought of a widow who might just do everything she could to make sure she did not live the rest of her life known as the woman of the man who had killed himself because he just couldn't handle his money. Would she rather live her life with *that* over her head, or with a constant outpouring of sympathy because her husband had been murdered—likely by someone jealous of his hard work ethic and wealth?

He reached under his desk and grabbed the small briefcase that he rarely used. He was more of a gun and badge sort of dick, staying away from anything more official. But he placed the financial documents in the briefcase, pretty sure Delia D'Amour would crack when she saw them. If he had this sort of damning evidence, surely she'd come clean.

He made his way out of the precinct and once again wished Ava were there with him. Not only was she better with approaching women suspects, but the phone call from her the previous night was resting heavily on him.

She'd called him late at night. She'd called him during a low point, when she was feeling lost. Sure, she claimed he'd been the second choice because her father and son had been sleeping, but he wasn't sure he bought that…not entirely, anyway.

That conversation, plus the fact that he felt somehow incomplete as he started his trip over to Delia D'Amour's residence, had Frank feeling uneasy in the best way possible. It showed him that he and Ava were starting to rely on each other. Their partnership at work had been brief (it had been just over a month, in fact) but the connection he felt was beyond just work. There was a romantic element there, sure, but maybe even something more. Frank had never been the best with making friends, much less girlfriends, because he had never taken the time to truly understand or appreciate dames.

But Ava was changing that. She was polishing off bits of him he'd left unattended while also improving some aspects of the way he worked—and that was the hardest part to admit to himself.

He hoped she was doing okay with her case. More specifically, he hoped she'd wrap it up soon and come back to her home precinct. Lingering above all of those hopes was the comment from the pocket of the banker who had dove off of a building a month ago, the blood-splattered paper in his pocket.

Money isn't worth this and truth be told, trouble is coming.

It felt foreboding, as if the man had been a fortune-teller rather than another tired, worn-down stockbroker.

Trouble is coming…

It wasn't exactly the sort of thing a detective wanted to hear as he walked through the streets of a city that seemed to grow every day. A city that was starting to affect the people who lived within it rather than the other way around.

CHAPTER TWENTY THREE

Ava knew she was at a disadvantage not only because she was a woman, but because she was a woman whom people were starting to hear about. Her last few run-ins with the mob and other shady individuals had proven that. Because of these things, she knew that it was going to be incredibly difficult to go back to the 77th precinct and just hang around. Her plan was to go back to the precinct and stake the place out for Officer Banner. She'd not dare engage him in the precinct, so she thought she could perhaps wait until he left and then follow him.

And if he took too long to leave, maybe she could get a good idea of some of the friendships he had within the precinct. Maybe, if she played her cards right, she could even discover what cases he was working on. One way or the other, she simply needed to find out if he was keeping secrets of any kind, and how he conducted himself on a day-to-day basis around the precinct.

But of course, being in the precinct and not drawing attention to herself was going to be tricky. As she walked from Amberley's apartment back to the precinct, she came up with a plan she thought might work. She tried to come up with reasons it might fail so she could work around them but, aside from her own potential negligence, she thought it should work. When she walked in through the doors, she kept her head down. She did not even bother to greet the pleasant woman sitting at the front desk. She made a direct path back to Captain Skinner's office and knocked on the door. She was greeted with the same monotone greeting she'd received the first time she'd visited the precinct.

"Yeah?"

She opened the door and poked her head in, making sure not to actually walk inside. She wanted to give him the impression that she was busy and on the move. "Sorry to bother you again, sir. But I wanted to get your permission to spend some time in your Records room."

"That should be fine. Do you think you have something?"

"Not sure, yet, honestly. I just want to have a look around to see if I can find any other reports on the deaths of journalists in the last few years."

He barely let her finish her statement before he was answering again. It was clear he just wanted her out of his hair—that she was nothing more than a nuisance that had been passed down to him from Captain Minard.

"That's fine. Just put everything back in its proper place when you're done."

"Yes, sir. Thank you."

She closed the door and made a disgusted expression. It had been harder than she'd thought to come off as a lousy, subservient dame. But she didn't care, because she had no intention at all of working in the Records room. As she walked away from Skinner's office, she slowly scanned the bullpen area. She recalled Banner's face from earlier in the morning, slightly young and with a confidence that had seemed quiet more than cocky. Short-cropped brown hair with a strong chin. She didn't see him right away, so she slowly walked around the bullpen and back to the front desk. She was aware of all of the stares she was getting but chose to ignore them. So long as no one was getting in her face and giving her a hard time, she could let it all slide.

As she walked back to the front desk, she again kept her head down for most of the walk but managed a few quick scans of those sitting at their desks and moving around the building. It was then, as she neared the front desk, that she spotted Banner. He was standing at the edge of another officer's desk, and they were looking over a series of photographs. She quickly made note of where he was and hurried to the front desk.

The lady behind it smiled at her warmly. "Can I help you?"

"Yes, I'm sorry," Ava said, showing her badge. "I'm Detective Ava Gold, helping with a case here. Where on earth is the Records room?"

"Do you know where Captain Skinner's office is?"

"I do."

"Well, you hang that right down the hall just off of his office. The Records room is the last door on the left down that hallway."

"Thanks so much," Ava said. This time, she hurried around the bullpen, glancing up only to see if Banner was still standing by that same desk. When she saw that he was, she made her way to the hallway the woman at the front desk had indicated. Seeing that there was currently no one moving around in the hallway, Ava turned back to the bullpen.

She cleverly moved about for the next ten minutes, keeping an eye on Banner. When she moved to the left to head to the restroom, she saw that he was still standing by the same desk. When she came out of the restroom and made her way back to the front desk with another question in mind, she saw that he was moving to the other side of the bullpen, where he sat down at his own desk. Ava then made her way to the breakroom as Banner remained at his desk. She knew she was continuing to get some unwanted glances, but that was to be expected, she guessed. But this was part of her plan, too. Later, some may even joke that she'd been moving about the building like a lost little girl, not sure where she was going or what was going on.

She came out of the breakroom with a cup of water when she saw Banner getting up from his chair He grabbed his jacket from the back of the chair and slipped it on. When he headed for the front door, he waved to another cop and said something with a laugh. She waited until Banner was nearly at the front desk before she started walking in that direction as well. She timed it perfectly, keeping her pace slow but methodical. By the time she had also reached the front desk, Banner was already out of the front doors. Before they closed, she saw that he was taking a slight angle to the left. She waited a handful of seconds and then also passed through the doors.

Outside, there was a fair amount of foot traffic on the street, but she spotted Officer Banner easily enough. He was heading to the east, walking at a brisk pace. With enough space already between them and at least a dozen or so pedestrians filling that space, Ava wasted no time and followed after him.

***

Ava followed with at least half a block between them. Banner walked for quite some time—at least half an hour easily—before coming to a stop. He'd walked in the same direction for most of the walk, heading into a quieter part of Brooklyn. The fact that he had not taken a cab or used a precinct automobile made her suspicious right away, though she reminded herself that this could easily be police business and nothing suspicious.

This was a bit harder to convince herself of when Banner turned down an alleyway that was almost completely hidden by the sheer size of the factory that served as the right side of the alley. It looked to have not been used in quite some time, the letters on the front almost completely faded. It had apparently been an old grain storehouse at one time. She walked by the alley first, casting a quick glance down it to see where Banner was headed. She crossed by just in time to see him disappear through a door on the side. He was moving quickly, and did not bother looking over his shoulder. This was a small godsend because if he had, he would surely have seen her.

Ava waited a few seconds before starting down the alley. As if to reassure herself, she placed her hand on her holstered Smith and Wesson before heading in that direction. When she came to the door Banner had passed through, she found it closed but slightly ajar. It was an old wooden door, partially swollen and buckled along the bottom so that it no longer sat fully in the frame. Using the slight crack between the side edge of the door and the frame, Ava peered inside. Again, she watched as Banner passed through a doorway, this time in a wall roughly ten feet away from where she stood.

She pushed the wooden door open and stepped inside. The place smelled of old grain and thick dust. She hesitated for a moment, knowing that going deep into a building she was unfamiliar with might be a very big mistake. But in her hesitation, she heard someone talking. It was a loud, boisterous voice that she did not think belonged to Banner.

"What the hell are you doing here this time of the day?"

"I've come to ask about my money." This definitely sounded more like Banner. Realizing that she was about to eavesdrop on a conversation, Ava stepped over against the wall the exit door was on. If this conversation went bad, she wanted to be as close to the door as possible. As she did, she took in more of the building's interior. There were a few more doors along the back wall, and all the way to the back, a single staircase that went up elsewhere. As far as she could tell, there was no one else in the building.

"Money?" the other voice said. "What makes you think I owe you money?"

"You gave me your word! You told me if I looked the other way on your bootlegging operation, you'd send me two checks. The first was delivered the next day. I'd like to know where my second one is."

The owner of the other voice laughed heartily at this. "First of all, you'll get it when I decided you've earned it. Secondly, you are just going to have to give me some time to sort it all out. I'm paying so many officers to look the other way—not to mention even doing some of them some favors—that it's hard to keep up with which coppers I owe money to."

"I don't give a damn about those other cops," Banner said. "If I don't have the rest of my money by the end of the week, I'll report it."

"Oh, you will? If you think you're the only cop that knows about it, you're a fool. You go public with it, I'll have at least two other cops to refute it. And they'll also warn me, and I can move. And guess who'll end up looking like the fool then, *Officer* Banner."

"And what about this dead reporter?" Banner asked. "I know quite a bit about that as well. Maybe I can start with that and steer the investigation towards your other endeavors."

"Officer Banner, I'd watch your threats. The reporter situation is becoming a very tense one. And unless you want a mob war on your hands, you may want to stay away from that case."

"A mob war over a dead journalist?" Banner said. "That seems like an overreaction."

"I agree. But Mr. Clay Johnson seems to think the bullet that killed Mille Newsom was intended for him. He thinks it was a hit attempt and if this story keeps getting attention, he's going to become obsessed with it. And all because of this meddling broad of a cop. What a joke."

"Well, *was* the bullet that killed the journalist an attempted hit on Johnson?"

The other man chuckled again, but there was no humor there. "Officer Banner, if you think we concern ourselves with the trivial writings of a—"

He was interrupted by the slightest of sounds. It came from somewhere overhead, making Ava looked immediately to the stairs to the right of the room the conversation was coming from.

"Damn it, Banner! Were you followed?"

"No, I—"

Ava could hear flurried movement coming from the room. She rushed to the door that led back to the alley, pushing her way through just as Banner and a second man came out of the room. She watched them rush up the stairs with guns drawn. She remained by the door, curious to see what happened next. Not only that, but the conversation she'd overheard seemed to be leading to answers she needed in order to wrap this case.

Several seconds later, she heard one of the men yell out: "No! You stay right there. Don't move an inch!"

She then heard the faint sounds of a skirmish somewhere overhead and then thundering footsteps heading back in the direction of the steps. When she heard the creaking of the stairs, Ava pulled away from the doorway. She pressed against the side of the building, waiting to hear an indication that she could peek back inside without being seen.

She listened as a few words were exchanged. It was mostly Banner and the man he'd come to meet, but there was a third voice mixed in as well—a scared, panicked voice.

"Who sent you?"

"No one! I was just—"

"That's horse shit! How did you even get upstairs?"

"You'd better talk." This was Banner's voice, sounding much more confident than he had when speaking to the man he'd come to visit. "Do you have any idea what you've stumbled into?"

"I'm sorry. Look, I don't—"

He was interrupted by a meaty slapping sound. Her years spent around a boxing read told Ava that this was the sound of a well-placed punch right across the face. Not only that, but just before the words had come to a halt, she thought she recognized the voice.

She chanced a quick glance inside just to see if she was right. When she looked inside, all three men were facing away from her, heading in the direction of the room Banner had appeared into when he'd first arrived. One of the men was holding his jaw—clearly the man who had just been punched.

"Idiot," Ava whispered.

It was Ronald Amberley.

CHAPTER TWENTY FOUR

Ava was furious. It was almost as if Amberley were trying to get himself killed. What the hell was he doing here? It was a question that could be answered later, she supposed. For now, her most pressing question was how she was supposed to get him out of this situation without making things infinitely worse for herself.

"No!" Amberley pleaded. "Please…"

Ava wasn't sure what he was referencing until she looked back to the other two men. The one who wasn't Banner—a man she was starting to assume was a mafioso from another group or family—had drawn a revolver. He was slowly inching toward Amberley's head.

"Well, this is the price to be paid for trespassing," he said. "For snooping."

"Whoa, hold on there," Banner said. "I can't be here for this. With my job, the last thing I need is being an accessory to this man's murder."

"Then get the hell out of here."

She knew in that moment, she had to make a choice. She could either make sure she saved Amberley's life, or she could wait for Banner to make his exit and capture him. She supposed she *could* try to do both, but it would be very risky.

Uttering a curse under her breath, Ava went back into the building. All of their backs were still turned to her, so she didn't bother announcing herself. Besides, the closer she could get to them, the better chance she had of successfully getting both tasks done. She hurried her steps a bit and by the time anyone heard her, she had gained more than enough ground.

Banner turned to face her first. She just barely saw his surprised look of recognition before she clocked him along the side of the face with her right hand. Holding the Smith and Wesson in that hand provided a bit more force to the punch but also caused her fingers to go numb for a moment.

As Banner went spiraling to the ground, the apparent mafioso turned his gun her way. But before he could get it level, Ava brought her elbow down on his wrist, stepped forward, and delivered a hard

114

punch to his kidney. The gun clattered to the floor and the unnamed mafioso hit the floor like a sack of rocks. He screamed out, mostly in pain, but with some frustration as well. Ava kicked his gun out of the way, the weapon skittering across the floor.

At the same time, Banner drew back around, bringing his gun up. He was angry and working on nothing more than adrenaline. His arm looked a little too loose when it came up. Seeing it come up and knowing what was coming, Ava hit the floor. The gunshot sounded out less than a second later.

With her heart hammering with the knowledge that she'd narrowly avoided death (maybe by just a few inches as far as she knew), Ava had to fight her instincts. Every muscle in her body, including her still-numb fingers, wanted to return fire. But even though Banner was clearly dirty, she could not imagine the amount of shit that would be heaped upon her if she killed a cop. She refrained from using the gun and, instead, threw out her right leg in a hard sweep. It was not a move she'd ever performed before—it wasn't used in a boxing ring, after all—so it was clumsy and hurt her more than it should have. It was effective, though, sending both of Banner's feet off of the ground.

He landed with a painful-sounding thud on the concrete. She saw his head hit quite hard and after a single groan, he stopped moving. Ava got up, prepared to turn around to do her best to nab the mafioso, but was shocked to find that he was already coming at her. He had drawn back an enormous fist and she had no time to block it. All she could do was turn her head away so that her ear and jaw caught the impact rather than her face. It sent her around in a hard spin. She nearly lost her footing, but managed to stay upright and assume a boxer's stance. But even then, he was already coming again. He delivered a punch to her chest which she blocked easily, but a right hook came out of nowhere and clipped her shoulder. She stumbled back, surprised by the man's size and strength.

As he charged again, she saw the hatred and anger in his eyes. She had no doubt that given the chance, he'd beat her to death with his bare hands. Before he could land another shot, though, she saw a flicker of movement over his shoulder. She watched, surprised and alarmed, as Amberley came up behind him. He held the mafioso's gun in his hand, holding it by the center and drawing back to use it as a small club.

Amberley struck the man on the back of the head hard enough to cause him to stumble forward and cry out in surprise. The moment his hand went to the back of his head, Ava took advantage. She fired off two rapid-fire right-handed punches. Both caught him in the face, one just above the bridge of the nose and the other in the chin. The sound of his teeth clinking together was almost like dishes being stacked.

He tottered for a moment and then hit the ground again. This time, just like Banner, he was showing no signs of movement.

Massaging her hand and wincing, Ava looked to Amberley. "You're a fool," she said. "What the hell were you doing here?"

"I wanted to know, too," he said, almost defensively. "I just wanted to he—"

"You were nearly killed! Jesus…would you just stay put? You're not a cop, not a detective! Right now, you're just a pain in my backside and you need to get out of here right now. Go home, Ronald!"

"But I—"

"No! Get your useless ass home right now before you end up getting us both killed."

There was a brief spark of anger in his eyes that was quickly washed aside by what she read as hurt. He hung his head, tossed the mafioso's gun to the ground, and headed out of the alleyway door. Watching him go, Ava wondered how long he'd been here. Had he arrived only seconds before she had? And if so, how had she missed the fact that he'd also been tailing Banner?

With Amberley gone, Ava looked to the two men she'd knocked out. At first, she had no idea what to do, but an idea suddenly occurred to her. She knew what she had to do. She was going to make more enemies and ruffle a few feathers, but she honestly didn't care. She'd tiptoed around more than enough people over the last day and a half, and she was done with it. She had a job to do and, by God, she felt she was doing a damn fine job of it.

She checked Banner's vitals, as well as those of the mafioso, and took away their weapons before hurrying out to the street. She had to rush to the end of the block, but was able to secure a cab within two minutes. Rather than get in right away, she stayed outside of the car, looking in at the driver.

"I need you to follow me down this street, to this old, abandoned building," she said. "I've got a bit of a load to carry with me." She hesitated for a moment and frowned. "And if you can help me lug some of it into your car, there will be a nice tip for you."

"What sort of a load are we talking about?"

116

Ava nearly chuckled before turning her back to him and starting down the street. "Just come on," she called over her shoulder as she ran back to the warehouse.

CHAPTER TWENTY FIVE

Ava hadn't had much of an issue hauling Banner into the back of the cab. He was rather skinny and didn't weigh all that much. It was quite the task to get the mafioso into the car, though. He was dead weight, though he was muttering a bit as she moved him. The cab driver did indeed help, though it was clear that he was uncomfortable with it. Ava gave him his tip up front and that seemed to ease him a bit.

The task was made easier by cuffing the mafioso but it was still grueling work. She was huffing and puffing pretty hard by the time she and the driver had both men in the back of the car.

She heard them both stirring slightly during the ride. In fact, by the time the cab was parking in front of the precinct, Banner had nearly come to. His eyes were opened but he was quite groggy. It looked as if he'd just returned from a long night of partying.

"Where are we?" he asked dreamily.

"Back at work," Ava said as she paid the driver. He looked very amused, looking back to the two bested men in the back.

Banner looked over to the mafioso and suddenly came to his senses. "No. Look, Gold. You don't know what you're doing."

"The fact that he's cuffed and you're just now waking up sort of shows that I *do* know what I'm doing."

"You can't do this," Banner said.

Ava ignored him and got out of the cab. She waved down a cop that was starting up the stairs. He looked at her with an uncertain smile and then to the cab. He looked confused, maybe wondering if he was part of some kind of joke or prank.

"Sorry," Ava said. "I've got two suspects in the cab and only one set of cuffs. Can I borrow yours? I'll give them right back when I get inside."

Clearly baffled, the cop nodded and slowly handed over his cuffs. He stood by as Ava went back to the cab. She opened the door and took a single step back when she saw that Banner intended to charge at her.

"Really?" she asked. "You want me to put you on the ground again in front of the precinct? Think of how many people would see."

"I'll have your badge for this," he hissed.

She ignored the comment and hauled him out. He fought a bit but when she twisted his arm behind his back, he yelped. She pushed him against the side of the cab and applied the cuffs. She heard the other cop coming down from the stairs in a hurry.

"Is that…is that Banner? You crazy dame, what the hell are you doing?"

Ava hitched a thumb into the back of the cab. Looking to the officer who had lent her his cuffs, she asked, "Any idea who that is?"

"No. What are you—"

"He owes Banner money for keeping quiet about a speakeasy. These two are in cahoots."

"Not Banner! He—"

"Would you give me a hand here? This other guy is pretty heavy."

"No way," the cop said. And then, just as confused as ever, he headed inside. She noticed that he was running, probably to tell Skinner about the scene currently taking place outside.

Irritated and now fueled mainly by the frustration of the past half an hour or so—from Amberley showing up again to the other cop refusing to assist her—she hauled the mafioso out of the cab. It took some shoving and cajoling but she finally managed to usher Banner and the mafioso in through the front doors. By that time, the mafioso had finally come around, likely spurred on by the movement of his legs as Ava led him up the stairs and through the door.

"What's this?" he said, still dazed. "How did I get here?"

Nearly every face in the building turned in Ava's direction. She looked to the back, near Skinner's office, and saw the cop who had handed over his cuffs. He was speaking to a very agitated Skinner and once the captain's eyes found Ava, he started directly across the bullpen. Piles of papers, reports, and other documents were flying from the edges of desks as he passed by.

Ava barely flinched. She stood her ground, despite the mafioso starting to struggle against her. His shoulders flexed as he fought against the cuffs that held his arms behind his back.

To Skinner's credit, he waited until he was standing directly in front of her before he laid into her. Ava was impressed; it showed great restraint.

"Gold, you'd better have a damned good reason for marching a *cop* through my doors in handcuffs."

"I do, sir. Several, in fact. The first being that he took a shot at me. The second being that he's apparently working to protect this other gentleman."

"And who is this?" Skinner asked, looking to the man.

"I don't have a name. But I did overhear a conversation about—"

"You have no business interfering in my affairs," the mafioso interrupted.

To Ava's surprise, Skinner got in the man's face. "That's for me to decide." He waved a nearby cop over. He was a large, older man. His name tag read THOMPSON. "Officer Thompson, please see this gentleman to a holding cell for questioning."

Thompson did as he was asked, stepping forward as if he'd just been called out onto a stage in front of hundreds of people. When he reached out to take the mafioso, the man recoiled a bit and Ava was sure there was going to be another fight. But Thompson put some muscle into it and finally pushed the mafioso along.

"Who is he, Banner?" Skinner asked.

"Sir, you can't honestly believe her, right? You know me! Do you really think I'd be wrapped up with some mobster?"

"I'd like to think not, true," Skinner said. "But I also know that Detective Gold has just about the entire world breathing down her neck right now. She wouldn't act on something like this if it would destroy her career." He then looked over to Ava and gave her an accusing stare. "Isn't that right, Detective Gold?"

"That's exactly right," she answered, not missing a beat.

"So for now, Officer Banner, I'd like for you to go to my office. Have a seat, wait for me, and we'll have a talk."

Banner nodded but it was clear that he did not like the idea. He looked out to the bullpen where his fellow policemen watched on. With his hands still cuffed behind his back, he walked to Skinner's office with his head hung in shame.

"As for you," Skinner said, his attention now back on Ava, lowering his voice. "There's a part of me that wants to thank you. I've suspected there were dirty cops in my precinct even before that nosy journalist started snooping around. But here's where I have a problem with this whole situation. Even if this mafia guy turns out to be guilty, and even if Banner *is* connected to him, you're still interfering where you have no business. Why were you sent here, Detective Gold?"

She knew where he was going with this, but she took the bait anyway. He had, after all, made a small step in standing up for her when the mafioso had spoken up. "To look into the death of Millie Newsom."

"That's right. You need to be looking for a killer…not going off on some misguided crusade."

"But the trail led me to—"

He interrupted her, his voice lower than ever now. "Detective Gold, I can tell you beyond a shadow of a doubt that Banner had absolutely nothing to do with the death of Newsom. Banner was here, in this precinct, when the murder occurred. And there's another thing…"

He paused here and looked around a moment. Placing a hand on her lower back, he led her closer to the front of the building, right by the front desk. "Based on your findings from yesterday, I sent a pair of cops out to where you said you found that speakeasy. And there was nothing there. Not a damn thing."

This shocked her, and she didn't bother trying to hide it. "That's impossible, sir. Did they look in the back room, beyond the supply—"

"They checked the entire place. Now they did say that they could see where it looked like someone had done some moving in the last few days—sort of left a bit of a mess behind. But still…there was nothing. You're running into these situations like you're invincible, Gold. Keep it up, you're going to wind up dead. And you're also going to make our jobs a lot harder. This so-called speakeasy for instance…we could have potentially shut it down and made some arrests had you not gone in there like some damned Wild West cowboy."

He had a point. She was still drenched in adrenaline and anger, but she knew he was right. She nodded and waited to see what else he had to say. She figured if he told her she was now off the case and he wanted her back in Manhattan right away, she'd understand.

He leaned in even closer, so close that she could smell his lunch on his breath. Something with pepper, for sure.

"I have no idea what to do with you at this point. I have never liked the idea of pulling a detective off of a case. So for right now, I think it's best that you just have a seat while I get Minard on the phone. Maybe he and I can come up with something."

She opened her mouth to argue but shut it right away. She didn't want to come off as if she were begging. Instead, she nodded and waited for him to turn away. She didn't even bother asking where she should have a seat. She simply walked around to the other side of the front desk and had a seat in the waiting area. And as she sat there, her stomach started to churn with regret and angst as she realized that while she sat idly by, two men would be having a conversation that would determine the course of her future.

CHAPTER TWENTY SIX

"Excuse me, but could I borrow a pen and a sheet of paper?"

The woman at the front desk gave Ava a look of approval and nodded. "Of course." She grabbed a sheet of precinct stationery and a well-worn pen from a drawer in her desk. As she handed the items across the desk, she added: "I know you're getting a lot of grief and angry looks from out in the bullpen, but I think what you're doing is incredible. I'd read about you in the paper, so to see you come in with those two men...it was nice. It was encouraging. So please...keep up the good work."

As conceited as it may seem, it was exactly what Ava needed to hear in that moment. It appeared that without the filter of macho skepticism, she was doing a good job. She tucked this away in her heart and it did wonders for staving off her frustration. She sat back down in the chair in the front waiting area and began jotting down thoughts and notes on the case as she knew it so far.

She still wasn't willing to rule out Banner, despite Skinner's statement. Millie Newsom had not only known of him, but written his name down in her notes and circled it. Where things got tricky, though, was in knowing just how connected he was to the mob and the mafia. Was he *only* running with the man she'd brought in, or was he linked to Clay Johnson, too?

In jotting down the names and places she'd so far been entangled with, she found herself coming back time and time again to Clay Johnson. While he'd seemed genuinely confused when Ava had mentioned Millie Newsom's name, the fact of that matter was that he was less than three yards from Millie when she'd been killed.

On her sheet of paper, she jotted down his name in the center. When comparing it to all of the other players, his was the only name that could not be eliminated with hard proof. If Skinner was right and Banner had been here in the precinct when Millie had been killed, that would rule him out.

Similarly, George Spotnitz had been occupied during her death as well. And it was becoming clear that the various mafia members involved with the speakeasy she'd run into yesterday were likely not part of it, either—not unless something huge came up when Banner's mafioso friend was questioned.

So maybe she just hadn't thought long and hard enough about Clay Johnson. After all, he was a criminal. Why in the hell had she taken his word for it so easily?

Or maybe it really was a case of Millie being in the wrong place at the wrong time, she thought. *Maybe she really was just caught in the crossfire of an attempted hit on Johnson.*

As she started crossing names out on her sheet of paper, a man came walking in through the precinct's front doors. Ava only looked up because she saw the motion out of the corner of her eye, and then looked right back down to her notes. She barely noticed the man walking to the front desk and when he spoke, she only registered it as background noise. But then he said something that grabbed her attention. Actually, it nearly caused her to drop her pen.

The man mentioned the name of Millie Newsom. Not only that, but he did it quietly. Ava didn't even take the time to think twice. She got up from her chair and hurried over to the desk. When she stepped up beside the man, he flinched a bit.

"You mentioned Millie Newsom?" she asked.

"I did. Who are you?" He was a middle-aged man who had the sort of slight droop to his face that made Ava wonder if he simply always looked perpetually sad. He was losing his hair up top and what remained was quickly going gray.

Ava showed her badge, keeping it low and on the desk so no one out in the bullpen would see her. "Detective Ava Gold. It just so happens that I'm running the lead on this case."

"Oh, I see."

Ava noticed the woman behind the desk smiling. But she said nothing and went on about her business.

"Did you have questions about the case?" Ava asked.

"No. I...well, I have some information I think might be useful. I mean...have you found the killer yet?"

"We have not. Sir, what's your name?"

"Cal Myers. I work in the shoe store across the street from where the shooting occurred."

She was excited about the prospect of this new break in the case, but had to remain skeptical based on the late delivery of the news. "And why have you decided to come forward so late in the case? It's been nearly two days."

124

"I know," Myers said. "I was scared. Whenever the mob is involved in that part of town, most people just turn a blind eye, you know? So that's exactly what I did. I saw what happened but got scared. I looked the other way. But ever since then, I haven't been able to sleep. I felt guilty. And after a while, the guilt turned into shame. The mob is getting away with these things so often *because* people keep turning their heads."

"How do you know it was related to the mob?"

"Well, because I saw the guy on the street. I recognized him. He doesn't really make it much of a secret that he's in the mafia, you know?"

"Who are you talking about?" Ava asked.

"I don't know his first name, but his last name is Johnson. He's always coming into businesses as if he owns the place. He purchased three new pairs of shoes from my store just last week."

"So you know his face well? There's no chance you might have mistaken him for someone else?"

"No. I know it was him."

"This is a huge help, sir, but I need to know exactly what you saw."

She led him to the chair she'd been occupying, as it was clear he was nervous to be giving this information. She stood by him and waited as patiently as she could for him to finally begin.

"I was out sweeping off my stoop when I heard the shot. I ducked down, as you would, you know? And when I looked over that way, I saw him. He looked a bit scared, too, and at first I assumed someone had taken a shot at him. But then I saw him…he was putting away his gun. Sort of stuffing it down into his coat."

"So he had drawn his gun?"

"Yes."

"And you're absolutely certain of this?"

"Yes."

"But you did not see him pull the trigger?"

Myers shook his head. "No, I never saw him pull the trigger. But what I do know is that he was putting his gun away. He was not pulling it out like he might be ready to return fire. He was *putting it away*. And then he looked confused for a split second and lay down on the ground as if he was just as scared as everyone else."

Gotcha, she thought. But before she could turn and run out of the precinct, she needed to know a few more things. Skinner was right; she'd been running almost blindly into some of these situations.

Besides, the account was too good to be true and she still remained hesitant to buy into it. The fact that Myers had waited so long made it a little hard to swallow, even if he *had* named Johnson specifically. Then again, even if she wasn't completely buying it, it was far too coincidental to ignore. Also, she knew she was only second-guessing it because of the scolding she'd just gotten from Skinner.

"Mr. Myers, you've done the right thing," she said. "And I can assure you that no harm will come to you because of this."

"Thank you. I'm…I'm just sorry I waited so long."

"It's understandable," she said. "Now, if he was apprehended and we needed your testimony, would you give it?"

"I suppose," he said, though he sounded terrified.

Ava gave a small nod and then headed for the door.

"Hold on, wait," Myers said. "That's it? Where are you going?"

"Well, I've got two days to make up for," she said, making sure to add just a bit of irritation to her voice. "I'm going to find Johnson."

***

Against her better judgment, Ava decided that she needed to pay another visit to Ronald Amberley before she went out looking for Clay Johnson. In the rush of trying to close the case and the rapid-fire appearance of one failed lead after another, there was a very important question that had still gone answered—and it was a question she thought Amberley would be able to answer. That was, of course, if he was still willing to speak with her after the way she'd berated him during her trailing of Banner.

She went by his apartment and knocked on the door. When he did not answer, she recalled how easily she'd been able to break in the first time she'd come here. But she wasn't going to do that this time. Even if he *was* home and was ignoring her, he had a right to do so. Besides, what sort of message was she sending if she told him to breeze off one moment and then went by to speak to him less than two hours later?

She knocked once more before giving up. She exited the building, wondering if Clay Johnson would possibly be at the same building she'd gone to before—the location of what was known as the Duck Pond. She had walked about half a block when a familiar voice called out from behind.

"It was very nice of you not to break in this time."

126

Ava turned and saw Amberley approaching from the other end of the block. Given the way his last few days had gone, Ava wondered if he was hesitant to say at home. Remaining on the move was surely the smartest option, but not very far away; that way he could keep an eye on his home without actually being there. It was a pretty smart move, she had to admit.

"Well, I didn't come suspecting you of murder this time," she said. They walked toward one another, meeting just shy of the door to the building.

"Did you come by just to make sure I was staying put?" he asked.

"Not exactly. Someone came into the station with a pretty solid tip on what likely happened during the shooting. But before I tell you what this witness claims, I need to know how you knew where to find Clay Johnson. You led me right to him, like you'd been there before."

"Yeah, you can thank Millie for that, too. That was the first place she wanted to check out for this story she was working on—whatever the topic might be. We hid out there one night for about an hour or two, just watching people coming and going. Clay came out on one occasion, and she pointed to him. 'That's Clay Johnson, big mobster figurehead,' she said. I asked her how she knew and she just chuckled."

"Did she know there might be a distillery there?"

"I don't think so, but with Millie, there was never any way of knowing. She'd never come out and say something was true or not unless she knew for absolutely certain. It's sort of important when you're a journalist."

"And a detective." She thought the story over and then asked: "Was that the only time you saw Clay Johnson?"

"No. One day Millie was out asking questions of local businesses, wanting to know if they ever experienced any mistreatment by the police. I figure it was another angle on her story where she was looking for evidence of dirty cops. As we were going along, we passed him on the street. She waited until we were well past him to point him out, though." He frowned as he recalled the memory before asking, "Now can I ask what you've found out?"

"I've got a witness stating that he was on the other side of the street when Millie died. He said when he turned in the direction of the shot, he saw a gun in Clay Johnson's hand. He claims Johnson was putting it away rather than pulling it out in self-defense."

"Oh my God," Amberley said hopefully. "How reliable do you think the story is?"

"Pretty reliable. Reliable enough for me to pay Johnson another visit, I think." She sighed, not liking what was about to come out of her mouth. "I know you felt strongly for Millie and that she was training you. I'm okay if you come along with me on this, but you *have* to keep a safe distance."

"Agreed," he said right away. "But are you only allowing me to come along so that I don't sneak behind you anyway?"

"Possibly. I'm serious, Ronald. You stay behind me the entire time. You're only coming to collect the story and take it to the paper. If there are dirty cops working with the mob to not only get booze out onto the streets but to also silence journalists that get too close, we need to get that story out."

"I can do that." He took a moment to consider what it meant, apparently just now realizing what they were about to do. "I've seen you kick some serious ass these last few days. But with the mob...you know they'll kill you if they get the chance, right?"

She did know this, and was doing a pretty good job of suppressing her nerves. But the comment stung, heaping even more weight on her.

"Yes, I know that. The trick is to just not give them the chance."

With that, she started walking back toward the end of the block, not bothering to turn around to see if Amberley was joining her.

CHAPTER TWENTY SEVEN

Ronald Amberley was beginning to think he just had a doomed disposition to be drawn to powerful, stubborn women. He'd pretty much been in love with Millie just before she'd died, and it had been a growing attraction born of respect at first, but then something much deeper and emotional. Now, as he followed Ava Gold back to the site of the so-called Duck Pond, he realized that he found her very attractive, too. She was very good-looking, sure, but it was her overall aura of toughness that he admired most. Because of it, he felt almost safe as they drew closer to Clay Johnson's Duck Pond.

It was nearing three o'clock when they came to the block. He noticed that Ava was looking up to the windows over the old abandoned department store and the surrounding businesses—the small diner, barbershop, and plumber's shop. Amberley eyed the windows, too. He'd wondered if Johnson might have upped his lookouts and security measures after Ava's first visit. But from what he could tell, things were still and quiet not only along the windows and storefronts, but the streets as well.

As they came to the end of the block, Ava turned back to him. He was a little taken aback by the stern look of determination on her face. If she was frightened about what they were planning to do, she wasn't showing it at all.

"You said you and Millie had been spying on the place for about two hours, right? I need you to show me where."

That was going to be easy. It had been one of the most nerve-racking nights of his life, as he'd been sure someone would sneak up behind them with a gun to their heads at any moment.

"Head towards the back lot, but keep walking to the end of that street. Hang a left at the end of the block." He almost asked if he could just take the lead, but knew she wouldn't allow it. So he followed along, feeling a slight tinge of eeriness at how similar it was to the late afternoon he'd followed Millie to the exact same spot.

His directions took them all the way to the other side of the block Clay Johnson's base of operations was located on. The parking lot that led to the Duck Pond was now out of sight, which brought him a little relief. But knowing where they were headed next made it disappear pretty much instantly.

"Halfway down the block, there's an alley," Amberley said. "You'll see an old wooden set of stairs leading up a second-floor apartment that hasn't been lived in for years. When Millie and I used it, we were pretty sure people had been squatting in it."

Ava asked no questions, following his directions perfectly. They walked down the thin alleyway, a rundown little strip of broken asphalt that showed signs of homeless occupancy and neglect. As they climbed the stairs to the apartment, the creaking of the wooden steps brought back another flash of memory from that night.

Damn, I miss that woman, he thought. As Ava came to the old, worn door of the apartment, he could almost see Millie in her for a moment.

Ava pushed hard against the door and it opened up with a whoosh of dust and the scent of stale air. It was a one-room setup and he saw some of the same trash that had been on the floor his first time up here: crumpled newspapers, some sort of old sandwich wrapper, and more mouse droppings than he cared to imagine.

Ava had already gone to the only window in the place. It was to the right, slightly cracked and almost completely caked in dust and grime. Looking out of it, he could remember Millie yelling at him for almost wiping the grime away. *"What are you doing?"* she'd scolded him. *"Do you want him to know someone is up here, looking out?"*

He noted that Ava didn't wipe the mess away either. She simply stepped up to it and peered out. Amberley did the same. Despite the dirty condition of the window, the view of the back of the old department store Clay Johnson was supposedly using as a distillery was in plain sight.

"I'll go ahead and ask the question," Amberley said. "Why are we staking him out rather than just going in after him?"

"We?" Ava asked. He wished there was a little more playfulness in her voice but as it was, she sounded quite serious.

"Okay, fine. Why aren't *you* just going in after him?"

"Because he may be expecting it. And if that's the case, we have no idea how many men might be in there. Quite frankly, my right hand is aching like crazy from all the fights I've been in over the last few days and I don't want to use it unless I absolutely have to. My hope is that I can catch him coming out on his own."

As she spoke, Amberley was looking out of the window and watched as the rolling loading door started to rise. "You might get your wish sooner than you thought," he said.

They both watched as a man came out of the large loading door. Because of the grime on the window, he had to get a bit closer before it was clear that it was not Clay Johnson. It was an older gentleman, dressed in a dapper fashion. He was carrying a bag very close to his side. Coming out of Johnson's supposed distillery, it was easy to imagine what might be inside the bag. Behind him, the door rolled back down. Amberley wasn't sure, but he thought he could just barely see a murky figure inside the opened doorway, cranking the door back down in its frame.

They stood there in silence for a moment, Ava staring through the window with such concentration that it almost looked like she was meditating. Never having been one to tolerate silence, Amberley broke it in a soft voice. He knew no one could hear them down below but it still seemed like a sensible precaution.

"You mentioned all the fighting you've been doing," he said. "Have you always been a good fighter?"

"Not always. But my dad was a boxer." She stopped, as if choosing where to go from there. When she picked it up again, she was nonchalant about it. "So I was unofficially trained in a boxing ring."

"Are you serious?"

"Yes. I know…a girl boxer seems ridiculous, doesn't it?"

"I won't lie…it does, sure. But it also fits you."

She smiled, never taking her eyes off of the parking lot down below. "My father always told me that, too." The smile remained on her face for a bit longer and when it did fall away, it happened all at once. She nodded to the window, where, on the other side down below, the loading door was coming open again.

Again, there was only one man. His head was covered in a rather nice fedora and the suit he was wearing was far too nice for pretty much anyone on this side of town. A few steps away from the building, and Amberley could see most of his face clearly. He was walking to the right, in the opposite direction of the customer that had come out roughly fifteen minutes ago. Even if the clothes weren't a dead giveaway, the identity of this man was clear. As if to confirm, Ava said it out loud.

"Clay Johnson."

At once, she moved to the doorway. She waited a moment and looked back to the door. "Is he out of the parking lot yet?"

Amberley looked through the window and watched as Johnson angled out of sight, heading to the very same alley he and Ava had taken to reach the apartment. "Yes. And coming right down our alley."

They both fell quiet as Ava pressed her head to the small crack between the door and the cracked frame. The tread of footfalls down the alley was faint but hard to miss. They drew closer, echoing slightly, and then started to grow dim. After a few more seconds, Ava pushed the door open. She held her index finger up, giving Amberley a *one second* gesture as she stepped out onto the stairs.

She then disappeared down them and he cringed at how loud they sounded. When she'd reached the bottom of the stairs, he made the decision to head out after her. He started taking the stairs down as he watched Ava quietly sprinting to the end of the alley where, apparently, Johnson had gone. By the time Amberley got to the ground, Ava had reached the end of the alley. She peered out to the right, paused a moment, and then drew her gun.

Amberley sped up as Ava rounded the corner, heading back onto the street out of his sight. He made it about five running steps forward when he heard the gunshot.

No, he thought. Instantly, he was back on the street where Millie had died. He'd been following a strong, determined woman, and he'd ended up being there by her side when she died. *No. Not again. I can't live through that again…*

He ran to the end of the alley, not realizing until he came to the end that Johnson could be waiting for him, too. He could come around the corner only to get a bullet in the head and—

When he came around the corner, he saw the exact opposite scenario. Ava was standing just a few feet away from the mouth of the alley. She was standing as rigid as stone, her gun drawn and pointed directly ahead. Roughly ten feet away, Clay Johnson was on his knees, his hands clasped to his stomach. His hands were covered in blood, the same dark also spreading along the white shirt under his suit coat. A dropped gun sat directly in front of him, splattered with blood.

"Ava?" Amberley whispered. "Ava, are you okay?"

It seemed she could not take her eyes off of Clay Johnson, or what she'd done to him. She nodded but Amberley wasn't buying it.

"He knew I was coming," she said, her voice and eyes both distant. "He knew I was coming and drew on me."

The way she was reacting made him wonder if this was the first time she'd ever shot someone. It was an alarming thought, one that keyed him in to the fact that he may need to act fast before this got out of hand or misconstrued some way.

"Okay," he said. "You stay there and I'll see if I can find some help."

As he turned and ran off, he heard Johnson groaning behind him but as far as he could tell, Ava was still some other faraway place, still standing as straight as a rod with her pistol still held out in front of her.

CHAPTER TWENTY EIGHT

Ava was still slightly rattled, and she couldn't remember much between firing the shot and arriving at the hospital. She knew that Ronald Amberley had flagged down another cop and that cop had called an ambulance. She was also vaguely aware that Skinner had been contacted and he was likely going to send someone to the hospital to meet her. Other than that, though, it was all blurry and fragmented in her mind. She believed she had taken a cab to the hospital (only because she remembered the driver telling her she needed to pay) and she was also pretty sure Amberley had gone back home at the prodding of the cop he'd flagged down once Clay Johnson's body had been moved.

Truth be told, Ava wasn't completely sure why she was currently sitting in the hospital waiting room. She simply done it because the other cop had asked if that's where she was headed next. As she recalled the moment, she was pretty sure it had been the cop who had secured the cab for her.

She shook the clouds of those memories away, trying her best to focus on the here and now. She sat in the waiting room, curious to see who might arrive first: someone from the 77th Precinct, or a doctor to give her an update on Johnson's condition. She wasn't all that surprised to find that it was neither. It turned out to be Ronald Amberley.

"I thought you were going back home," Ava said.

He took the seat beside her, an ugly stiff-backed chair with about a dozen of its twins occupying the waiting area. "I did. Took a shower and had a cup of tea. Let's be honest…did you really expect me to stay put?"

"No, not really."

"Ava, how long have you been a detective?"

She almost didn't answer him because it was a puny truth. But it came out easily and she really didn't care what he thought about it. "Right at a month."

"That's it?"

"Yes. That's it."

"I don't mean that as an insult," he said. "I would have never guessed. You're pretty amazing at what you do." He paused here and asked: "Is that the first time you've ever shot someone?"

She nodded. "It feels strange, but it feels even stranger to know that had I been half a second slower, it could be me in one of these hospital rooms."

"Do you think you're going to be okay?"

She nodded, though her thoughts were on Frank, Jeffrey, and her father. She could not remember a time in her life since she'd been a little girl when she'd wanted to be home so badly. She almost spoke up to say something about how she appreciated the help he'd provided, but she never got a chance. She noticed a cop coming into the waiting area. He spotted Ava and walked over to her instantly. She thought she recalled his face from the precinct when she'd been staking out Banner. He was a man of average height and build, the sort of face that tended to blend into a crowd. The nameplate over his left breast read BELL.

"Detective Gold, I'm Detective Bell, with the 77th Precinct. Captain Skinner sent me down to stand guard at the suspect's room. He also told me to ask if you feel safe. Do you need an escort to leave?"

"Thanks, but I think I'm fine. I know it may sound odd, but I'm going to stay here until I can get an update on Johnson."

Bell nodded. "Well, I'm sure there will be a few other dicks to show up. If you change your mind about that escort, let me know. I'm not particularly keen on standing guard outside of a hospital room."

"Thank you, Detective Bell."

He gave a little nod and left the waiting area.

"Seems the guys at the precinct respect you," Amberley said.

"Oh, if it were only that simple."

Amberley seemed to think very long and hard about something. They sat in silence for several moments before he rubbed at his head as if trying to push away a headache. "I'm trying to make sense of this," he said. "So it was him all along? You were right there, standing inside that building he's using as a distillery, and it was him. He shot Millie to keep her quiet, to keep her off of a story that would make him look bad, and then painted the picture to look like someone was trying to off him."

"Seems that way. And it's a very smart move. It eliminates the threat of the negative publicity *and* makes him seem very important. I mean, if you're in the mob and someone is wanting to knock you off, you must be a big deal."

Amberley shook his head in disgust. "What a bastard."

As Ava nodded her agreement, a very hurried-looking doctor walked into the room. When he spotted Ava, he walked directly to her. "You're Detective Gold, yes?" he asked.

"I am."

"Detective Bell told me you'd want an update. I have a preliminary one that I expect to remain the same with no huge changes. Mr. Johnson is going to live, though there's going to be a surgery or two to repair some damage the bullet did to his small intestine. He's currently stable, but under sedation. So if you're wanting to speak with him, I'm afraid you're going to have to wait."

"I understand. Thank you."

As she watched the doctor walk away, she thought about something she'd told Amberley several minutes ago. *It feels even stranger to know that had I been half a second slower, it could be me in one of these hospital rooms...*

Yes, if she'd been slower, Johnson would have gotten the drop on her and it would have all ended very differently. She thought of him on his knees, losing blood. She thought of his gun lying at his feet. She did not know the make or model, but she did know that it had been somewhat large.

She sat up in the uncomfortable chair as an uneasy feeling tore through her. She pictured the blood-splattered gun, recalling how badly a shot from something so large would likely have hurt.

But then her mind flashed to the visit she'd paid to the coroner. She'd looked at the bullet that had killed Millie Newsom. The coroner told her it had looked to be a fairly common round. And what else had he said?

"Small caliber, from a handgun. Most likely a revolver."

In other words, it was not the same sort of gun that had killed Millie Newsom. Sure, someone like Clay Johnson likely had many guns, but it was casting enough doubt in her mind to make her wonder.

"Ava?" Amberley said.

"Yeah?" she said as she got to her feet.

"You okay?"

"Yes. But I need to check on something. I'll try to catch up with you later, okay?"

She was rushing out of the waiting room before he said anything. She hurried to the front door and was moving so quickly that she nearly collided with Captain Skinner at the front door.

"Gold! What's the hurry?"

She made the decision to not tell him her suspicions with lightning speed. If she did tell him, it would only slow things down and cast her under an eye of scrutiny. "Just overwhelmed, sir. Anxious to get out of here, to tell you the truth."

"I suppose so. Damn fine job today, Gold. Really. It nearly makes me forget the fact that you disobeyed a direct order. I did ask you to stay seated and wait for Minard and I to speak, right?"

"Yes, sir. You did."

He waved it away and sighed in a way that she thought was supposed to be humorous but came off as almost offensive. "I won't mention it if you won't. Now, I've already taken the liberty of calling Minard and informing him. As far as I'm concerned, I can have one of my men do the write-up. I'll happily call you a cab if you need it."

"Thanks, sir, but not right now. I'd like to see it to completion but right now...I just need a moment."

"Of course. Whatever you need. See you soon?"

"Yes, sir."

She tried to seem composed as she passed through the doors and out into the large hospital parking lot. She passed by a young man pushing an elderly lady in a wheelchair, then hurried by someone angling a Model T into one of the many parking spots. She barely noticed any of it though. Her mind kept focusing on the gun that had fallen in front of Clay Johnson after she'd shot him, and the bullet that had been taken from Millie Newsom's body. And the further she got away from the hospital, the more certain she became that she may have made a very big mistake.

***

The coroner seemed almost happy to see her again, though Ava doubted it was her individually. She supposed in his line of work, any visitor who still had a heartbeat was a welcome change. And though he seemed a bit chatty when she met with him in his office, Ava made it clear that she was in a hurry.

"I've got a pressing question I need answered, and I think it might be directly related to the bullet you showed me the first time I was here. Do you mind getting it again?"

"Of course. Hold on one second."

Picking up on her urgency, the tall man moved swiftly out of the office. Ava heard him clamoring around not too far away from his office, opening up the same drawers he'd gone through the first time she'd visited. He came back less than a minute later with the small envelope. He handed it to Ava and she opened it right away, dumping the spent round into her hand.

"You said you'd guess that this came from a small caliber gun, right?" she asked. "Maybe a revolver?"

"Yes. And I still believe that to be the case."

"Are you certain?"

He considered his answer for a moment and when he finally spoke, his words were slow and calculated. "I deal in dead bodies. I'm not a weapons expert by any stretch of the imagination. But I do see a lot of gunshots come through here. And that is a very common type of bullet."

"I'll level with you right now," Ava said. "I'm only familiar with two types of guns. I have a personal weapon that belonged to my husband. It's a Colt...a forty-five caliber, I believe. The other is the Smith and Wesson I carry for the force."

"Well, I am quite certain this bullet came from neither. It resembles a lot of gunshot wounds that I've seen that come from what are known as pocket pistols. These are smaller caliber—some revolvers and some in a semiautomatic build. They are usually quite small, hence the name. They are easier to conceal. I mean, it *could* be a Smith and Wesson, but it would be much more compact than your sidearm."

"So you believe Millie Newsom was killed with a smaller gun. Maybe even with one of these small-bodied pocket pistols?"

"Yes. Again, I'm not an expert. But based on roughly forty or fifty gunshots I've seen in the past eight months or so, I'd bet my house on it."

Again, Ava saw Clay Johnson's handgun on the street—a handgun that had not been small at all. In fact, it had been a bit larger than her Smith and Wesson sidearm. And just like that, Ava knew she got the wrong man. Some may think it a bit of a stretch; after all, he could have just used a different gun. But based on what she'd seen and heard of Johnson, the idea of him using a small gun—or a small *anything* for that matter—didn't line up. Wouldn't he carry the same gun, a gun he was familiar with, in most dangerous situations just for that familiar feeling of safety?

What it meant was that Clay Johnson—though guilty of many things—was not Millie Newsom's killer.

"Thank you," Ava told the coroner as she got up.

She knew where she needed to go and she even hoped that if she got there soon enough, there might be plenty of time to correct her mistake.

CHAPTER TWENTY NINE

Ava was starting to feel as if she were single-handedly keeping all of the cabbies in New York City in business. She'd lost count of how many she'd used since starting her job as a detective, but she did know that it was starting to hit her finances a bit. Of course, her finances were the last thing on her mind as she paid yet another cab driver and ran back into the 77th Precinct.

She realized it was crazy what just a few hours could do. The last time she'd come in, she'd been reprimanded by Skinner and could still feel the stinging stares of privileged men. Now, based on how Skinner had treated her back at the hospital, she had no fear as she raced to the front desk. She hoped word had spread and finding help wouldn't be the chore she feared it might be.

She started at the front desk, approaching the woman she'd seen so many times over the last two days but to whom she'd never been properly introduced. "I'm so sorry to keep bothering you," Ava said. "But do you know whatever became of the man that was in here earlier…the one I spoke to just as he came in?"

"Well, he left pretty soon after that. I did ask him to meet with another officer so we could get his information."

"Which officer was that?"

"I believe it was Officer Thompson." She pointed over into the bullpen to where Thompson was sitting.

Ava thanked the woman and made a direct line to Thompson. He was currently filling out a bit of paperwork. He had his head down and was intensely focused on whatever task he was doing.

"Officer Thompson?"

When he looked up, he seemed uncertain how to feel about her standing there. There was surprise, shock, a bit of fear, and then a sort of knowing smile. "Hello, Detective Gold. We all heard about what happened with you and Clay Johnson. I do hope you're okay."

"I'm fine, thank you. But I do need to speak with the gentleman that came in earlier with the tip on Johnson. The lady up front said you took down his information. Is that right?"

"Sure is," he said. He instantly went to a small stack of papers on the right side of his desk, neatly sorted into a metal tray, and plucked a sheet out. He handed it to her and then slid a pen and pad of paper her way.

She recalled his name before she read it on the report: Cal Myers. Jotting down the address, she asked: "Do you have any idea how long it's been since he left?"

"Oh, it was pretty much right after I took the information. So maybe two hours ago."

She looked to the address and chuckled at herself. Like an address would do any good. She knew next to nothing about Brooklyn, especially how to get around. She supposed she could give the address to yet another cabbie if it came down to it. And then, just as she was about to ask Officer Thompson where the address might be located, she noticed that Myers had put down his work address, too.

Not that she needed it. He'd told her exactly where it was. After all, it had really driven his story home and made it more believable. Sliding the paper back to Thompson, Ava was already on her way back across the bullpen. She felt like she was running a very elaborate race. She was no longer only being pushed by her need to close this case, but she also felt she needed to rectify the mistake she'd made with Clay Johnson. Yes, it had been a case of shoot-or-be-shot, but the situation itself would never have arisen if she'd not gone back to the Duck Pond with the sole intention of tracking and then confronting him.

So once again, she hailed down a cab. She'd seen the name of Myers's business on the report, so she gave it and the address as soon as she was sitting down. "Myers's Shoe Store," she said, following it up with the address.

It was eerie to think this was the third time in the past two days that Ava was heading to the site of Millie Newsom's murder. As she wondered why Cal Meyers would have reason to lie to the police, she also watched Brooklyn roll by. It was odd how similar it was to Manhattan, but different all the same. Knowing that it was all linked by bridges and roads gave her one of those consuming realizations that this city was just becoming too damned big.

As they drew closer to the address, Ava recalled something Myers had said. At the time, it had made all the sense in the world. It had been so convincing that he'd somehow managed to hide a subtle truth in his grander lie. He'd mentioned how men like Clay Johnson came through the stores and businesses from time to time, acting as if they owned every store they stepped into. He talked about how most people in those neighborhoods knew of Johnson and other men like him. While he did not come out and say it, the whole story made Ava think Myers feared Clay Johnson. But the truth was a little plainer to see, really. Now, with almost full certainty Clay Johnson was not the killer, it was clear that Myers was covering for someone. The remaining questions, of course were *who* and *why?*

These questions were chiming in Ava's mind when the cab pulled to the corner. She also felt more of that frustration setting in as she headed for the door to the shop. Cal Myers had lied to her. More than that, he had sent her after a member of the mafia and she'd then shot that man. God only knew what that was going to mean in the coming days. She already had a hard enough relationship with the mob as it was.

She entered the shoe store and a little bell chimed over her head. The store was small but well-kept. A small front counter separated the front of the store from a dozen or so short aisles lined with shoes. The small shop smelled of leather, wax, and shoe polish. A pleasant older lady stood behind a counter, flipping through a ledger. She looked up at Ava and smiled warmly.

"Help you, dear?"

"Yes ma'am. I'm looking for Cal My—"

She saw him step around a corner in the back, carrying a box of shoes. He was reaching up to return the box to one of the shelves when his eyes landed on her. His face went rigid and his eyes grew wide. He froze like a deer having heard the snap of a twig on the forest floor as a hunter approached.

"Hello again, Mr. Myers," she said. She did her best to keep her voice calm and even but the anger was there, too. "I need to ask some follow-up questions about your testimony."

"Oh," he said. "Well, if you…I mean, I can—"

If he'd been a frozen deer before, he now took off like that same woodland animal, terrified for its life at the intruder into its natural habitat. He dropped the box of shoes and took off at a mad dash toward the back of the store. Ava took off after him without pause, even though she could feel the fatigue and stress of the last two days wearing heavily on her body.

She squeezed around the front counter and gave chase. She only caught the briefest glance of the elderly lady. She looked genuinely confused, having no idea what was going on. As Ava got to the back of the shop at the end of the rows of shelves, she saw a door to the right. Beyond it, there was a light and the sound of rapid footfalls. She headed in that direction and went into the room just in time to see a back door closing, slowly blocking off the alleyway beyond. The room she found herself in appeared to be a stockroom, but she didn't take any time to study it. She hit the back door before it had time to close fully. When she came to the alley, she saw Cal Meyers several yards ahead. He was running at a good pace and when he looked over his shoulder and saw Ava behind him, he seemed to find another gear.

As Ava continued to chase him down, she watched as he came to the end of the alley and crossed a street. She heard the squealing brakes of an automobile, as well as two distinct voices yelling for Myers to watch where the hell he was going. Ava didn't miss a beat, running as fast as her legs would carry her. She came to the sidewalk and the street Myers had crossed just as she watched him disappear down another side street.

"Myers! Don't make this harder on yourself!"

He either didn't hear or didn't care, because he did not reappear. Ava crossed the street and took the same side street he'd taken. There were a few people on this street, most huddled around the entrance to a small delicatessen. Myers was slowed slightly when he bumped into a large man smoking a cigar, but he only stumbled a bit and then regained his footing. It was enough of a blunder to allow Ava to close the gap between them, though. Myers chanced another look over his shoulder and, in doing so, made his second blunder in a row.

He did not see the man hurrying across the street. The approaching man halted at the last minute and seemed to understand what was happening. He extended his leg in an almost nonchalant fashion, and Myers collided with it. He was moving with such great speed that he went sprawling at least five feet forward before colliding with the sidewalk. Ava heard him make a pained *oof* as she closed the distance.

Just before she fell on him, she took note of the man who had tripped him. She wanted to be angry, but a smile spread across her face all the same. It was Amberley. Of course, it *had* to be Ronald Amberley.

"You're absolutely ridiculous," she said as she hauled Myers to his feet. The comment had been meant for Amberley, but was appropriate for either of them, she supposed.

Amberley assumed it had been for him. "Whether you like it or not, you and I make a good team."

"Were you following me again?"

"Maybe. You're pretty easy to follow, if you want to know the truth. That, or I'm very good at tailing people. You have a partner back in Manhattan?"

"I do. And I think he'd fight you to make sure you're not competition for him."

"I'm sure he would," Amberley said appreciatively.

Ava had no handcuffs, having already used them on Officer Banner's mafioso buddy earlier in the day. *My God, was that today? How much longer could this day possibly be?*

She held him against the wall and she could already tell he wasn't going to put up much of a fight. His legs had gone to jelly and he was already on the verge of crying.

"You lied to me, Mr. Myers. Didn't you?"

"I don't know what you're talking about."

"I went after Clay Johnson based on your tip and he's currently in a hospital, needing surgery on his intestines. I have enough evidence to suggest he had nothing at all to do with Millie Newsom's death. Now...if it should get back to Johnson's friends that it was *you* that fingered him, you may not have many days left to really even worry about it. Catch my drift?"

"You don't understand!" Myers bellowed. They'd attracted quite a crowd but Myers seemed oblivious to it and Ava paid them no mind. Amberley was the only one that seemed to have noticed at all, as he was currently waving people around the impromptu interrogation.

"Try me," Ava said. "Help me understand."

"A few hours after the reporter was killed, he came into my shop! He told me that he'd need me to tell a certain story...to make it look like it was Clay Johnson."

"Who?" Ava asked.

But Meyers was already on a different topic of conversation and seemed to not have heard the question. "I told him no way, no way was I going to get involved in anything like that. But then he told me he'd pay me....that he'd pay me very well. And he *did!* Two hundred bucks to say that I saw it all go down, that it was Clay Johnson! I figured it was some easy money and it would also be one less mobster on the streets. I had to! Can't you see that?"

"Listen closely, Mr. Meyers," she said. "I need to know who came in to pay you off. Was it someone in a competing mob group?"

"No. No, it was a cop."

144

"Who?"

"I don't know his first name," Myers said, tears and mucus running freely now as he wept. "All I know is his last name because it was right there on his uniform. Bell."

Ava's blood went ice cold. She pushed Myers hard against the wall and pointed her finger at him as she started to walk away. "Don't go too far away anytime soon," she warned. "You're going to be questioned again about all of this."

Amberley raced over to her, confused. "What is it? Where are you going?"

Truly beginning to wonder if this day would ever end, she said, "I have to go back to the hospital."

CHAPTER THIRTY

Detective Richard Bell was rather amazed at how much of a mess this entire ordeal had become. More than that, though, he was also amazed at just how easy it had been to pull guard duty for the freshly wounded Clay Johnson. No one ever wanted this sort of duty so when he volunteered for it, Skinner had been delighted. The stupid asshole had always been pretty easy to fool.

And speaking of stupid assholes, he also couldn't believe that the incompetent chick detective had almost done the job he'd originally been asked to do. He still didn't know the full story, but his visit to that imbecile Cal Myers had been just in the nick of time. Ava Gold had apparently been *right there* when Myers came into the precinct and she'd bought his story without a single doubt. After that, the details got muddy because no one had really gathered all of it from Gold yet, but what was important was that Johnson had been shot in the guts and was currently behind the hospital room door Bell was standing in front of.

He was waiting for the doctor to come by and do his final check. The fellow was the talkative sort and had given Bell every possible update. The doc had no real idea how long the sedation would last, and that was fine with Bell. He couldn't care less when Johnson woke up. He just needed the doctor to get lost so he, Bell, could go into the room and finish the job.

Bell was still very embarrassed that he'd missed the shot three days ago. It was almost as if Clay Johnson had *known* he was there, hiding behind that parked Model T on the other side of the street. Bell was still convinced he couldn't have missed the bastard by any more than six inches. The bullet, of course, had ended up finding that nosy reporter, Millie Newsom, and caused a whole world of trouble. After that, Bell had begged to right his wrong and he'd been given this chance—this last chance by feared mafioso Pete Costello. Bell had no delusions about his current situation; if he screwed this up again, he'd be dead. They might find his body in the Hudson a few weeks from now with bricks in his pockets, or behind a dumpster somewhere with a few holes in his head.

He just needed the doctor to leave. He'd thought about going in to do it anyway, but it would be far too easy for them to trace it back to him. He figured that after the doctor left, it would be a good two or three hours before a night nurse checked on Johnson. And two or three hours would be plenty of time for him to split. And if Skinner ever asked why he left his station, he could easily just say Gold came by to relieve him. If it came down to who was lying, he knew Skinner and all of the dicks at the 77th would have his back—and probably some of the jerks down at Gold's precinct, too. From what he understood, she didn't have many fans down at her own precinct.

As he stood in front of Johnson's room on the second floor with his arms crossed and his hands itching to finish the kill, a nurse walked by. She was young and had a body like a vase and when she smiled at him, it nearly broke his concentration. When she passed by, she walked with a bit of swagger, as if to let him know he was very much aware that he was watching her go.

He shook his lust away, again focusing on this last chance he'd been given. Pete Costello would not give him another chance. Whether Bell liked it or not, he essentially belonged to the mafia now. It had started when he'd been tapped by some of Costello's men during an alcohol delivery out of one of Costello's distilleries. The deal was simple: if he looked the other way and worked to assure the men on the force that Costello was clean, he'd receive kickbacks on what Costello earned every month. It was a small stipend based off of what Costello made, but the monthly kickback nearly matched what he made at the precinct. But then when the rival group started to get more powerful, Bell's greed and opportunistic side reared their heads. Bell had approached Clay Johnson, telling him the deal he had with Costello, letting him know he'd be willing to do the same for Johnson's outfit. It had all gone well until Costello found out and—

The stream of consciousness was broken when Bell saw the doctor coming down the hallway. "My God," the doc said. "You look like a statue."

"Part of the job, I suppose," Bell replied.

"I'll take one last look at him before I head out for the day. I doubt anything has changed, though."

Bell stepped aside and let the doctor in. When the door closed behind him, Bell clenched his hands into fists. Before Millie Newsom, he had never killed a man before, though he *had* shot two people in the line of duty. He was fully prepared to do it again, mainly for his own survival, but he had not been expecting this level of nerves and…well, if he was being honest, excitement.

After all, Millie Newsom had been an accident. That made it almost *easier* to prime himself up to take Johnson's life. So he stood there, like a statue as the doctor had said, and waited. Apparently, the doctor was in a hurry to get home because he came back out less than two minutes later. He stood at the door for a moment, scribbling something down on a clipboard he held in his hands.

"He's showing signs of coming around a bit," the doctor said. "Some people respond differently to the sedative, so it's hard to tell. I do know that when he comes to, he's going to be in a lot of pain. So I'm putting a note here that it's okay for him to get some pretty intense pain relief medicine. One he gets that, he'll be rather loopy. I'd suggest your men trying to speak to him right between when he comes out of this current state and before he takes any pain meds. I'm also making a note here to allow the police to question him…to the point of reason. As backwards as it seems, his care does come first."

"Of course," Bell said. "Thanks, doc."

The doctor gave Bell a supportive clap on the back and then made his way down the hallway. Bell remained still for another five minutes, making sure the doctor or one of the nurses wouldn't come back for one last check or because they forgot something. After those five minutes, when the hallway was empty with the exception of an elderly man snoozing in a chair outside of a room at the other end of the hallway, Bell reached behind him and opened the door.

He pushed it open and stepped inside quickly. He then closed the door and turned to look at the man in the bed. Clay Johnson was very much still out of it, lying on his back and motionless. His body from the waist up was exposed, the rest of him covered by the bedsheets. Bell could see where the doctors had wrapped him up, the gauze and bandages tinted red. A small table sat by the edge of the bed, holding a pitcher of water and a steel bedpan.

But Bell wasn't concerned with that. Instead, he went to the head of the bed and pulled the pillow out from underneath Johnson's head. As he gripped it tightly in his hands, he looked down to see the rise and fall of Johnson's chest as he breathed deeply.

For the briefest of moments, he wasn't sure he could do it. But then he tried to imagine the things Pete Costello might do to him if he didn't come through. It would be a painful and very slow death for sure.

It was all the motivation Bell needed. He lowered the pillow. But just as he placed it on the mafioso's face, something moved behind him. He wheeled around, the pillow nearly forgotten, and uttered a curse as he reached for his holstered sidearm.

***

Ava raced through the hospital, flashing her badge at every desk she passed by so she wouldn't be stopped. She made her way to the end of the first-floor hallway and took the stairs up to the second floor. In the back of her mind, she was pretty sure she was going to be far too late. She was fully prepared to get to the door of Clay Johnson's room only to find that Detective Bell had left.

As she came into the second-floor hallway, she saw that the room—located on the opposite end of the hall—was no longer being guarded. Rather than be discouraged, she continued to the room. She supposed there was a small chance that Skinner had instructed Bell to stay inside the room now that the day shift was over. She slowed her pace a bit as she came to Johnson's door. Either he was not going to be inside or he *would* be—and either option was going to make for an awkward situation.

She opened the door and though her eyes saw the scene clearly, she could not instantly make sense of it. It was almost comical in a way, causing her to freeze up for a split second. She saw Bell standing by the head of Clay Johnson's hospital bed, holding a pillow. It was ridiculous because the first thing she thought was that Bell might be readjusting the pillow, making sure Johnson was comfortable. But by the time she knew that made no sense—when she knew he was in fact preparing to suffocate Johnson—Bell was wheeling around like a man who had been caught red-handed. He threw the pillow down and instantly reached for his sidearm.

Ava, though, had already been waiting for a tense situation, so she drew her own sidearm with equal speed. They matched one anther almost perfectly and Ava realized she'd somehow ended up in a stand-off. Her finger seemed to want to squeeze the trigger impulsively, recalling the terrifying moment she'd had with Clay Johnson less than three hours before. She'd come here just to confront the man, to tell him that his little payout to Cal Myers has been exposed—yet here she was, holding a gun on a man again.

"Detective Gold, lower your weapon."

"You lower yours first. Think smart here, Bell. You have no realistic way out of this. I caught you red-handed."

"I've got the advantage here," Bell said, though he sounded a little uncertain. "I can shoot you and claim you provoked me. I can say you'd come to finish Johnson off. And they'd believe me." He smirked at her and said, "Think about it, Gold. Who is going to believe you over me?"

"Maybe quite a few people, actually. Do you know how easily I got Myers to fess up? I know you paid him off to tell me that fake story."

This seemed to surprise and irritate him. He took a step closer to Ava, now about halfway down the length of the bed and with no more than five feet between the two of them. "Who have you told?"

"That's going to be my little secret for now," she said, hoping he took the bluff. She understood that the only way for this to end was for one of them to shoot. The fact that she'd entered to see him on the verge of suffocating Johnson had her wondering what other pieces to the story she might be missing. She had no idea what was pushing Bell, what was driving him to do these things, so she could not assume she could talk him down. He might be just as willing to kill her as he'd been willing to kill Johnson.

"Bell, there's no way this ends well for you," she said. "Drop your weapon and let's talk this out."

"No. I think I'll shoot you and take my chances. I don't think you've told anyone at all. If that were the case, you wouldn't be here alone. I think you—"

Ava had been so focused on Bell and his gun that she barely saw the movement behind him. Her eyes trailed over to Johnson's body for just a second—just long enough to cause Bell to turn his head the slightest bit.

The motion Ava had seen was Clay Johnson reaching for the small table at the side of his bed. By the time Bell had started to turn, Johnson had grabbed the steel bedpan and started to raise it. Bell brought his gun around but wasn't able to fully turn before Johnson slammed the bedpan into the side of his head.

Johnson cried out with the effort, the hard bowl obviously straining his injured abdomen. The clanging noise the bedpan made against the side of Bell's head was almost musical, the impact sending Bell stumbling back a single step. Ava took advantage at once. She pivoted forward, went low to put as much force into her knees as possible, and brought her entire upper body back up, channeling the force of the movement into her right arm.

The uppercut caught Bell directly on the chin. His head rocked back and struck the far wall of the room. As he rebounded, gun still in hand, Ava could see that the punch had disoriented him. She threw out a left-handed jab that finished him off. He fell to the ground in a gasping heap. She looked over to Johnson, her hand a ball of pain, and waited for him to speak first. But he looked washed out, the effort from his bedpan blow having sent shudders of pain through his body.

Ava went back to the door and opened it. She stuck her head out into the hallway and yelled, "I need some help here, please!"

She then checked Bell. He was still conscious, trying to get to his feet. Ava delivered a kick to his ribs that sent him back to the floor and once he was there, he seemed content to just stay there. He was gasping with pain but Ava turned her attention to Johnson instead. And as a handful of nurses came rushing into the room, she found herself hoping he had not aggravated the injury too badly. Although he was a criminal, he was also a man she'd falsely chased down for murder. If he died from this gunshot, the blood would be on her hands.

Slowly, Ava backed out of the room and made her way to the small nurses' station in the center of the hall. As she leaned against the counter, she realized just how tired she was; her arms were trembling and she was starting to feel very light-headed

"I need to use your phone, please," she told the young, tiny woman behind the counter. "I need…"

"You look faint," the woman said. "I can make the call if you like. Who should I call?"

"Police," Ava said, closing her eyes against the swimmy-headedness. "Call the 77th Precinct and ask for Captain Skinner."

The nurse nodded and Ava just barely heard the woman asking the operator to put her through.

CHAPTER THIRTY ONE

The second floor of the hospital was a chaotic scene for the next hour or so. On two occasions, Ava thought she was going to pass out. She remained by Johnson's door as several nurses went in and out. She remained there until Skinner and Officer Thompson arrived. When Skinner and Thompson took over, a kind nurse escorted Ava to a small breakroom where she provided a cool cup of water and a chocolate bar. Ava accepted both and sat there until each one was gone. She'd found the offering of a chocolate bar a little odd but was surprised to find that the sugar and overall flavor helped to clear her head and give her an extra little bit of strength.

She watched through the door as a few other cops arrived on the scene. What she also noticed, though, was she had not yet seen Detective Bell led out of the hospital in handcuffs. This made her nervous because she couldn't help but wonder if the other cops were buying his story.

Feeling stronger and confident enough to take part in whatever tasks were taking place, she refilled her water cup and started to head back to the hallway when Skinner appeared in the breakroom doorway.

"How are you feeling?" Skinner asked. "One of the nurses said you seemed a little out of it."

"I guess I was. It's been a very long two days."

Skinner nodded as he came into the room, sitting down at the same table Ava had been occupying. "I'm sure it has," he said. "And I apologize for not making it any easier."

Ava shrugged the comment off, looking out into the hallway. "What's going to happen to Bell?"

"You mean after he has the two teeth that got chipped because of your punch removed? He's going to spend some time in a holding cell and then go to trial."

"So he confessed?"

"More or less. Clay Thompson attested to Bell's guilt. He says he's got at least three others that can back him up. He also mentioned a mafioso named Pete Costello, and that's when Bell broke. He confessed to quite a bit. It seems he was working as a sort of hush-man for both mafiosi, and Pete Costello did not take too kindly to it. Costello blackmailed him and said he'd out him to the cops unless he showed his loyalty."

"That loyalty being to murder Clay Johnson?"

"Seems that way. But, and even Bell admits this, the hit went wrong and he got Millie Newsom instead."

"Are there others?" Ava asked. "Dirty cops, I mean?"

Skinner frowned at this but nodded. "I hate to think it's true, but Bell says there are. He hasn't given names yet, but I suppose it's just a matter of time. When he goes to trial, I'm sure some deals will be made—giving up names for a lesser sentence, that sort of thing."

Ava didn't like the idea of this, but she wasn't *that* naïve. She knew how the system worked. She was about to comment on this when there was a knock at the opened door. She looked up and was not at all surprised to see Ronald Amberley standing there.

"Hey there, Mr. Amberley," Skinner said. "You're fine to come in. I'm done." He looked back to Ava as he got to his feet and gave her a sincere smile. "I'm going to make sure everyone at your precinct knows the amazing work you did here. As far as I'm concerned, you're welcome at the 77th anytime."

"Thank you, sir."

Skinner left the room, and Amberley took his seat. "I want to point out that I was not following you. I just happened to be at the hospital, waiting for an update, when I saw a large number of police vehicles entering the parking lot. I simply came in for the story but was not at all surprised to find that you were part of it."

"So did you get the story?"

"Oh yeah. And I think Millie would be proud. I even got a quote from Captain Skinner, where he states…" He paused here and pulled a small notebook out of his back pocket. He thumbed to a certain page and read from it. "'After this devastating development, we'll be working hard internally to make sure there are no other cops that are putting their own interests above that of the public. If need be, we'll be cleaning house.'"

"That's one hell of a quote."

"I know. Now let's just see if he sticks to it."

"I think he will. And you know what? I'm happy for you, Ronald. Seems like you'll be able to fill Millie's position without much of a problem. Just, do one thing for me, okay?"

"What's that?"

"Stay out of trouble."

"I make no promises." He looked to her for a few moments and the stare reminded her slightly of how Frank sometimes looked at her. She felt herself blushing, so she looked away. "So what about you?" he asked. "What comes next?"

Ava gently massaged her hand, grimacing. "First, I'm going to get some ice for my hand. And after that, I just want to go home."

CHAPTER THIRTY TWO

Ava opened the door to her apartment a little shy of 9 o'clock that night. She'd only made it two steps into the kitchen before Jeffrey came rushing at her. He was in his pajamas and smelled strongly of soap. She'd apparently gotten home just in time for bed.

"I missed you!" Jeffrey said, hugging tightly to her leg. "We were worried, too!"

"I know, baby. And I'm so sorry."

"Did you win?" Jeffrey asked.

"Win?"

"Against the bad guys. Grandpa said you were out fighting with bad guys, and that's why you've been gone for two days."

She laughed weakly and said, "Yes, I suppose I did. And I missed you, too, you know. Are you about to go to bed?"

"Yeah. Grandpa said he was going to give me a few more minutes just in case you came home!"

As she hugged her son, she saw her father walking into the kitchen from the living room. There was a smile on his face but it was hiding something a little less joyful. "Good to see you," he said.

"And it's good to be back home."

"You okay?"

"Yeah. Just very tired." She looked at Jeffrey and said, "Is it okay if I sleep with you tonight?"

"Yeah!"

"Sounds like a plan. Why don't you go ahead and hop in bed? I need a shower, and maybe a word or two with Grandpa. Give me a few minutes, okay?"

Jeffrey gave her a big, sloppy kiss on her cheek and ran off to bed. She was relieved to find that he was happy to have her home rather than worried and asking her questions about why she'd been gone for so long. She wasn't sure she'd get that same treatment from her father, though.

Roosevelt came into the kitchen and sat down at the table. "If you're hungry, there are a few flapjacks left over from dinner. They're sitting in the oven."

"I probably should eat, but I'm just so tired, Dad."

"You sure you're okay?"

She grinned and showed him her hands. The right one was slightly swollen and the knuckles were red. "I know it's nothing to brag about, but I really wish you could see some of these men I'm knocking around. I think you'd be proud."

"I *am* proud," he said. "But I have to say this, despite how it makes you feel: I need you to start thinking about Jeffrey. I don't mind stepping in at all. We have a great time and it's easier to fall back into this parenting role than I thought it would be. But he needs a mom, you know? And this is at least the third time in a month where I've had cause to be concerned for you."

"I know, Dad. And I appreciate everything you're doing. I hope you know that."

"I do." She thought there was something else on his mind. She could see it weighing on him, wanting to come out. But instead, he grinned at her and looked back to her hands. "So do you have time to tell me about at least one of these fights before you go to bed?"

She instantly thought of the moment with Clay Johnson, having to shoot him before he ended her life. Of course, she wasn't about to tell him that story, though. Instead, she told him about taking on the three men in the Loose Goose. His wide grin helped speed the tale along and as odd as it seemed, that was how she knew he was proud of her.

With the story over, there was an unspoken understanding between them—an understanding that stated she was done talking about the details of this case with him. He was fine with it, and so was she. Yet, as she showered and got ready for bed, she realized she needed *someone* to share these things with. And if not her father, then who?

Unsurprisingly, her thoughts turned to Frank. He remained in the forefront of her mind until she crawled into bed with Jeffrey. There, every piece of her was centered on her son. She wrapped her arm around him and was asleep in just a matter of seconds.

***

Because of the way the last two days had gone, Ava did not feel the least bit guilty about arriving at work nearly an hour late the following day. She made her way down to her desk in the WB offices and after getting congratulations, applause, and mock whistling (this coming only from Lottie) she found the small note in the center of her desk.

She picked it up and read it, the message of it making her feel as if she was in the middle of some sort of shift when it came to her career and how people saw her. The note was brief and simple:

I'll be in Brooklyn most of the day, talking with Skinner about Bell's trial and what your involvement may need to be. As for you, take it easy today. Write up the case report and call it a day for all I care. I want to touch base with you first thing tomorrow morning, though. GREAT job, Gold. Clarence would be proud.

Cpt. Minard

She tucked the note away to glance back on later, maybe to perk herself up during a bad day. It was not the sort of thing she'd ever thought to hear from Minard. With the note stored safely away, she ventured upstairs. When she saw Frank sitting at his desk, hunched over paperwork of some kind, her heart warmed more than she cared to admit.

She walked over to him and place her still-sore right hand on his shoulder. "Hello, Detective Wimbly."

When he turned to face her, his smile was wide and genuine. The cheer in his eyes also alarmed her. It told her without a doubt that she was eventually going to fall for him. If she was being totally honest with herself, she thought it may have already started happening. It was a hard fact to swallow, though, with Clarence having been gone for less than three months.

"Detective Gold! It's good to have you back with us."

"Is it?" She looked out across the bullpen. She was not getting the usual angry and suspecting glares but the few stares she *did* get were uneasy. In her two days away, something had changed—and not necessarily for the better.

"Well, it is for me, anyway. I don't give a damn about the rest of them for right now."

"So what were you working on while I was gone?"

"A case that presented as a murder case but turned out to be a suicide. A rich stockbroker. Looking into it really opened my eyes. He frowned and added: "I feel like there's something bad on the way. So many of those rich folks offing themselves...it's odd."

"Were you able to solve the c—"

"Excuse me, Detective Gold?"

They both turned and saw one of the patrolwomen from the Women's Bureau. Ava was ashamed that she could not recall her name. Sherry or Sharon, or something like that. "Yes?"

"I thought you might want to see this," Sherry or Sharon said, handing Ava a copy of the day's paper. Only, it wasn't a paper she usually saw in this precinct. No, it was a copy of the *Brooklyn Eagle*, and the headline made her heart skip a beat.

AVA GOLD OUTS CORRUPTION IN BROOKLYN PD!

"Looks like you're just getting more and more famous," Frank said.

She nodded, not liking the feel of it as she scanned the article. Every detail of it was right. The only thing that rubbed her the wrong way was how heroic it all made her sound. She supposed Minard would be thrilled with it but something about it didn't sit right with Ava. The only thing that cheered her about the entire article was the byline. She grinned when she saw Ronald Amberley's name.

Done with the article, she looked back out over the bullpen. "How many of them do you think have read it?"

Sherry or Sharon shrugged as she moved away from the desk. "I don't know. Not many of us read the Brooklyn paper."

"Thanks for sharing," Ava said, turning the paper over to hide the headline.

"You okay?" Frank asked.

"Yeah, I think so." But what she was really thinking was that any hope of keeping her links and run-ins with the mafia was now pretty much impossible. She was going to live a risky life from here on out unless something changed very soon.

"So here's what I'm thinking," Frank said as he got up from his chair. He slipped his hat and coat on, gathering up his badge. "I have to go speak with a few people about this suicide. The case is pretty much closed, but this is just clean-up. I'd love to have lunch with you. You think that's possible?"

"Absolutely. Meet me at Lancaster's at noon?"

He smiled and gave her a nod. It was the sort of gesture that made him seem like a gushing teenage boy rather than a man pushing past forty. Ava picked up the newspaper and carried it with her back to the WB offices. As she settled in behind her desk, she started to gather together paper and a pen to start jotting down notes on the Millie Newsom case so she could then go upstairs to type it up. She figured she could have it done by lunchtime and then call it a day after lunch with Frank. She could pick up Jeffrey from school and maybe even take him to the candy shop.

As she started to write, another sheet of paper just to her left caught her eye. She put the pen down and looked it over. There were only a few words jotted down on it, all in her own handwriting: *wide-brimmed hat, short man, Clancy's?* The name of the old, retired restaurant had been circled. It had been the last list she'd made before investigating the place and discovering the devious acts hidden behind its walls.

She'd helped rescue that poor girl and she had since been taken to an orphanage. After getting that bit of good news, she'd been shipped off to Brooklyn and had been consumed with the Millie Newsom case. In all of that chaos, she'd nearly forgotten that her investigation into Clancy's had given her another lead into her husband's death that she'd not yet looked into. A man by the name of Floyd Lance—a man who was about to do God only knew what with that young girl she'd rescued.

Suddenly, the Millie Newsom report was the furthest thing from her mind. She left the WB office and headed upstairs. As she made her way to the Records room, she noticed a few cops looking at her. Again, she wondered how many had read Amberley's article. How many of them may be dirty cops or even contemplating such a choice? If there were even a few among them, they could be resentful.

Or afraid of you, she thought.

She made it to the Records room without a word spoken out against her. She stood there for a moment, looking at the cabinets and drawers. There were a lot of them—almost enough to overwhelm someone who had never seen it before. But she was slightly familiar, having used the set-up before.

Still, it took her a while to find what she was looking for. Rather than searching by date, she started flipping through old reports by name. She figured she'd then cross-reference any report with Floyd Lance's name with the date of the arrest. After several minutes, she started to worry she may not find a single thing, that Lance was the sort of crafty criminal who somehow never got caught. But her patience paid off and she ended up finding two reports featuring Floyd Lance.

The first was from nearly two years ago. Floyd Lance had been arrested for his involvement in a public brawl where he'd put a man in the hospital. He did two weeks of jail time for the crime and then, just four months ago, he was arrested again. This time, it was for suspicion of involvement in the kidnapping of a fifteen-year-old girl. She read through the report and found that he'd been let go for insufficient evidence. While reading the report, she also found that two other men had also been arrested and let go. She looked at the photos related to the crime: the mug shots, as well as four photographs from the arrest scene.

One of the pictures in particular caught her attention immediately. Standing beside the man she recognized clearly as Floyd Lance was a man of small stature, wearing a wide-brimmed hat low on his head.

She knew it wasn't an automatic ID on the man who had killed Clarence, but it certainly did fit. The man was a good foot shorter than Lance, the sort of man who was just short enough so that it would be the defining characteristic for someone trying to describe him. It was the exact description she'd been given for the man who had shot and killed her husband almost three months ago in a botched robbery.

She scanned back through the report, now ignoring the name of Floyd Lance. She went to the mugshot photos and found the picture of the short man. Without the hat in the mugshot, she was not surprised to find that his face was quite menacing. His eyes were small, dark, and lacking remorse. She looked to the informational plate and saw his name: Jim Spurlock.

But just as she saw that name, she saw another on the informational plate. It brought tears to her eyes and caused her to run her finger across the photo. At the bottom of the plate, she read: *Arresting Officer – C. Gold.*

C. Gold. *Clarence Gold.*

It felt much stronger than a coincidence. It stirred her so badly that she instantly started digging through Records for a man name Jim Spurlock, but it appeared as if the night he'd been caught with Floyd Lance had been his only arrest. It made her wonder, though, how many of the reports in the Records room were incomplete in a way—maybe listing a small man in a wide-brimmed hat as a suspect or person of interest, not knowing that it could very well have been Jim Spurlock.

A very strong sense of duty filled her as she looked back to the mugshots. She looked at Floyd Lance because he apparently had a history of abducting young girls. She had seen this firsthand but because of her reason for being out at Clancy's, she could not officially do anything about it. Not yet, anyway.

She then looked at Jim Spurlock, staring right into those dark, uncaring eyes in the photo. A creeping certainty took hold of Ava as she picked the picture up and studied it closely. She felt it like some new instinct, as if the finger of the universe were poking and prodding, letting her know beyond a shadow of a doubt that this was him.

This was the man who had killed Clarence.

CITY OF GHOSTS
(An Ava Gold Mystery—Book 4)

1920s. New York City. When a second immigrant woman turns up murdered in the Lower East Side, Ava Gold, the city's first female detective, is summoned to crack the case. But this serial killer is savage, and Ava's dangerous game of cat and mouse may just lead her too close to home.

"A MASTERPIECE OF THRILLER AND MYSTERY. Blake Pierce did a magnificent job developing characters with a psychological side so well described that we feel inside their minds, follow their fears and cheer for their success. Full of twists, this book will keep you awake until the turn of the last page."
--Books and Movie Reviews, Roberto Mattos (re Once Gone)

CITY OF GHOSTS (An Ava Gold Mystery—Book 4) is a new novel in a long-anticipated new series by #1 bestseller and USA Today bestselling author Blake Pierce, whose bestseller Once Gone (a free download) has received over 1,000 five star reviews.

In the rough streets of 1920s New York City, 34 year-old Ava Gold, a widower and single mom, claws her way up to become the first female homicide detective in her NYPD precinct. She is as tough as they come, and willing to hold her own in a man's world.

Ava fights an uphill battle to get her precinct to take the murder of an immigrant woman seriously. But Ava refuses to give up, and when the case leads only to dead ends, she's forced to take matters into her own hands

Could her own husband's murderer hold the secret to cracking the case open? And if he does—can Ava delve into her own past and catch the killer in time without being pushed to the edge?

A heart-pounding suspense thriller filled with shocking twists, the authentic and atmospheric AVA GOLD MYSTERY SERIES is a riveting page-turner, endearing us to a strong and brilliant character that will capture your heart and keep you reading late into the night.

Books #5 and #6 in the series—CITY OF DEATH and CITY OF VICE—are now also available.

Blake Pierce

Blake Pierce is the USA Today bestselling author of the RILEY PAGE mystery series, which includes seventeen books. Blake Pierce is also the author of the MACKENZIE WHITE mystery series, comprising fourteen books; of the AVERY BLACK mystery series, comprising six books; of the KERI LOCKE mystery series, comprising five books; of the MAKING OF RILEY PAIGE mystery series, comprising six books; of the KATE WISE mystery series, comprising seven books; of the CHLOE FINE psychological suspense mystery, comprising six books; of the JESSE HUNT psychological suspense thriller series, comprising nineteen books; of the AU PAIR psychological suspense thriller series, comprising three books; of the ZOE PRIME mystery series, comprising six books; of the ADELE SHARP mystery series, comprising thirteen books, of the EUROPEAN VOYAGE cozy mystery series, comprising four books; of the new LAURA FROST FBI suspense thriller, comprising six books (and counting); of the new ELLA DARK FBI suspense thriller, comprising nine books (and counting); of the A YEAR IN EUROPE cozy mystery series, comprising nine books, of the AVA GOLD mystery series, comprising six books (and counting); and of the RACHEL GIFT mystery series, comprising six books (and counting).

An avid reader and lifelong fan of the mystery and thriller genres, Blake loves to hear from you, so please feel free to visit www.blakepierceauthor.com to learn more and stay in touch.

BOOKS BY BLAKE PIERCE

RACHEL GIFT MYSTERY SERIES
HER LAST WISH (Book #1)
HER LAST CHANCE (Book #2)
HER LAST HOPE (Book #3)
HER LAST FEAR (Book #4)
HER LAST CHOICE (Book #5)
HER LAST BREATH (Book #6)

AVA GOLD MYSTERY SERIES
CITY OF PREY (Book #1)
CITY OF FEAR (Book #2)
CITY OF BONES (Book #3)
CITY OF GHOSTS (Book #4)
CITY OF DEATH (Book #5)
CITY OF VICE (Book #6)

A YEAR IN EUROPE
A MURDER IN PARIS (Book #1)
DEATH IN FLORENCE (Book #2)
VENGEANCE IN VIENNA (Book #3)
A FATALITY IN SPAIN (Book #4)

ELLA DARK FBI SUSPENSE THRILLER
GIRL, ALONE (Book #1)
GIRL, TAKEN (Book #2)
GIRL, HUNTED (Book #3)
GIRL, SILENCED (Book #4)
GIRL, VANISHED (Book 5)
GIRL ERASED (Book #6)
GIRL, FORSAKEN (Book #7)
GIRL, TRAPPED (Book #8)
GIRL, EXPENDABLE (Book #9)

LAURA FROST FBI SUSPENSE THRILLER
ALREADY GONE (Book #1)
ALREADY SEEN (Book #2)
ALREADY TRAPPED (Book #3)
ALREADY MISSING (Book #4)

ALREADY DEAD (Book #5)
ALREADY TAKEN (Book #6)

EUROPEAN VOYAGE COZY MYSTERY SERIES
MURDER (AND BAKLAVA) (Book #1)
DEATH (AND APPLE STRUDEL) (Book #2)
CRIME (AND LAGER) (Book #3)
MISFORTUNE (AND GOUDA) (Book #4)
CALAMITY (AND A DANISH) (Book #5)
MAYHEM (AND HERRING) (Book #6)

ADELE SHARP MYSTERY SERIES
LEFT TO DIE (Book #1)
LEFT TO RUN (Book #2)
LEFT TO HIDE (Book #3)
LEFT TO KILL (Book #4)
LEFT TO MURDER (Book #5)
LEFT TO ENVY (Book #6)
LEFT TO LAPSE (Book #7)
LEFT TO VANISH (Book #8)
LEFT TO HUNT (Book #9)
LEFT TO FEAR (Book #10)
LEFT TO PREY (Book #11)
LEFT TO LURE (Book #12)
LEFT TO CRAVE (Book #13)

THE AU PAIR SERIES
ALMOST GONE (Book#1)
ALMOST LOST (Book #2)
ALMOST DEAD (Book #3)

ZOE PRIME MYSTERY SERIES
FACE OF DEATH (Book#1)
FACE OF MURDER (Book #2)
FACE OF FEAR (Book #3)
FACE OF MADNESS (Book #4)
FACE OF FURY (Book #5)
FACE OF DARKNESS (Book #6)

A JESSIE HUNT PSYCHOLOGICAL SUSPENSE SERIES

THE PERFECT WIFE (Book #1)
THE PERFECT BLOCK (Book #2)
THE PERFECT HOUSE (Book #3)
THE PERFECT SMILE (Book #4)
THE PERFECT LIE (Book #5)
THE PERFECT LOOK (Book #6)
THE PERFECT AFFAIR (Book #7)
THE PERFECT ALIBI (Book #8)
THE PERFECT NEIGHBOR (Book #9)
THE PERFECT DISGUISE (Book #10)
THE PERFECT SECRET (Book #11)
THE PERFECT FAÇADE (Book #12)
THE PERFECT IMPRESSION (Book #13)
THE PERFECT DECEIT (Book #14)
THE PERFECT MISTRESS (Book #15)
THE PERFECT IMAGE (Book #16)
THE PERFECT VEIL (Book #17)
THE PERFECT INDISCRETION (Book #18)
THE PERFECT RUMOR (Book #19)

CHLOE FINE PSYCHOLOGICAL SUSPENSE SERIES
NEXT DOOR (Book #1)
A NEIGHBOR'S LIE (Book #2)
CUL DE SAC (Book #3)
SILENT NEIGHBOR (Book #4)
HOMECOMING (Book #5)
TINTED WINDOWS (Book #6)

KATE WISE MYSTERY SERIES
IF SHE KNEW (Book #1)
IF SHE SAW (Book #2)
IF SHE RAN (Book #3)
IF SHE HID (Book #4)
IF SHE FLED (Book #5)
IF SHE FEARED (Book #6)
IF SHE HEARD (Book #7)

THE MAKING OF RILEY PAIGE SERIES
WATCHING (Book #1)
WAITING (Book #2)

LURING (Book #3)
TAKING (Book #4)
STALKING (Book #5)
KILLING (Book #6)

RILEY PAIGE MYSTERY SERIES
ONCE GONE (Book #1)
ONCE TAKEN (Book #2)
ONCE CRAVED (Book #3)
ONCE LURED (Book #4)
ONCE HUNTED (Book #5)
ONCE PINED (Book #6)
ONCE FORSAKEN (Book #7)
ONCE COLD (Book #8)
ONCE STALKED (Book #9)
ONCE LOST (Book #10)
ONCE BURIED (Book #11)
ONCE BOUND (Book #12)
ONCE TRAPPED (Book #13)
ONCE DORMANT (Book #14)
ONCE SHUNNED (Book #15)
ONCE MISSED (Book #16)
ONCE CHOSEN (Book #17)

MACKENZIE WHITE MYSTERY SERIES
BEFORE HE KILLS (Book #1)
BEFORE HE SEES (Book #2)
BEFORE HE COVETS (Book #3)
BEFORE HE TAKES (Book #4)
BEFORE HE NEEDS (Book #5)
BEFORE HE FEELS (Book #6)
BEFORE HE SINS (Book #7)
BEFORE HE HUNTS (Book #8)
BEFORE HE PREYS (Book #9)
BEFORE HE LONGS (Book #10)
BEFORE HE LAPSES (Book #11)
BEFORE HE ENVIES (Book #12)
BEFORE HE STALKS (Book #13)
BEFORE HE HARMS (Book #14)

AVERY BLACK MYSTERY SERIES
CAUSE TO KILL (Book #1)
CAUSE TO RUN (Book #2)
CAUSE TO HIDE (Book #3)
CAUSE TO FEAR (Book #4)
CAUSE TO SAVE (Book #5)
CAUSE TO DREAD (Book #6)

KERI LOCKE MYSTERY SERIES
A TRACE OF DEATH (Book #1)
A TRACE OF MURDER (Book #2)
A TRACE OF VICE (Book #3)
A TRACE OF CRIME (Book #4)
A TRACE OF HOPE (Book #5)

Made in the USA
Coppell, TX
19 January 2022

71897269R00098